When A Man Wants A Woman

BY ARYA PHOENIX

Copyright © 2015 by Glass Slipper Media

All rights reserved. No part of this publication may be reproduced, distributed or transmitted in any form or by any means, including photocopying, recording, or other electronic or mechanical methods, without the prior written permission of the publisher, except in the case of brief quotations embodied in critical reviews and certain other noncommercial uses permitted by copy-right law.

Publisher's Note: This is a work of fiction. Names, characters, places, and incidents are a product of the author's imagination. Locales and public names are sometimes used for atmospheric purposes. Any resemblance to actual people, living or dead, or to businesses, companies, events, institutions, or locales is completely coincidental.

Phoenix, Arya
   When a man wants a woman/by Glass Slipper Media and Arya Phoenix
      ISBN-978-1-522-83741-1

Dedication

To Min. Joseph W. Burgess, Sr. and Mrs. Kimbley Reece-Towers.

I thank you from the very bottom of my eternally grateful heart.

It was because of you that I learned being covered in dirt is not always a bad thing.

How else is an acorn ever to sprout and grow into a great and mighty oak if it is never planted and buried in the ground?

Thank you both for planting and watering me.

Chapter 1
The Proverbial Wrong Turn

The yellow dress clung to Gigi's every curve. It had to if she was going to sign Black Ice. Evan Beauchamp was the R&B group's handsome, beefcake front man and he'd requested a dinner meeting with her.

His weakness was a beautiful woman and Gigi was going to play on that weakness to accomplish her mission. Their discography was still popular with the fans and they were about 10 years outside of their heyday but she desperately wanted Black Ice.

"Poor thing", she thought to herself.

He hadn't a clue she didn't find men like him attractive. She had a job to do and if flashing a little tit and ass was what she had to do to get the job done then tit and ass was what she was going to give him. There was only one thing Gigi Haralson wanted from the likes of *that* playboy: his band on her tour.

Men like him, men with money and a little power and influence thought every woman wanted them. The truth was most women really couldn't resist men like that and wouldn't reject them. She was not that kind of weak woman. He would be in for a rude awakening this evening if he expected anything else regardless of how much T and A she displayed.

She bent down to zip her Louis Vuitton boots just as the doorbell rang. She wasn't expecting company and didn't have time to entertain so whoever it was she had to get rid of and quickly. She grabbed her clutch from the bed, scooped her Yorkie up from the floor, dropped him into his cage and ran to answer the door.

She looked through the peephole and smiled. It was Chance.

She met Chance Williams online shortly after her divorce was final at www.lookingfortherealthing.com and they became an item immediately. The problem was she realized early that she enjoyed *fucking* him more than she enjoyed fucking him more than actually being with him and broke things off but continued to break him off every chance she got. If his freak game hadn't been so amazing, she may have been able to walk away clean but as it stood, she let him dine at her table any time he liked. A girl didn't come across sex that made your mouth fall open with no sound coming out of it often and when she did, she didn't let it go too easily.

"Chance, baby I'm afraid now is not a good time" she said when she opened the door

"Not a good time for this" he questioned and closed the door behind him.

He pushed her against the wall and fell to his knees as she willingly allowed him to find his favorite spot beneath her skirt.

"Two things I know about you, Girl. I know your freaky ass ain't never got on no panties and I know you always down for some of this good ass head" he said in between licks.

"Ooo Chance, that shit is good" she grumbled and sucked in air.

She tossed her leg over his shoulder, arched her back against the wall and thrust her hips forward towards his face to give him better access to her honey pot. She rested her hand on top of his head and grinded her pussy against his skillful tongue. Inaudible groans escaped her wide open mouth. She shook herself back into reality and tried reluctantly to take her leg down from his shoulders.

"As good as this shit feels and trust me it feels amazing, I really can't. I have an important meeting in 20 minutes and I can't be late but can I take a raincheck" she moaned and reluctantly climbed down off of his shoulder.

"You sure you want me to stop" he questioned and continued to suck, "because you know my shit is rock hard right now, don't you? You know I wanna replace this tongue with this dick right" he winked and pulled her back to him.

"Chance, baby I gotta go. I've got to meet Evan Beauchamp of Black Ice but meet me back here tonight and I swear I'll take care of you, okay? I got you later, I promise."

He stood and kissed her so deeply she was momentarily lost in the depths of his passion.

"That's what you taste like" he said as he pulled away. "11 o'clock, I'll be gone by 11:05."

Gigi saw Chance out, ran upstairs and took a quick whore bath then grabbed her coat from the closet. The doorbell rang again and she wondered what Chance had forgotten to tell her this time. That man was always finding a reason to come back after he left.

She flung open the door without looking through the peephole and found an attractive limousine driver at the door with a beautiful, shiny black, stretch Lincoln sitting just over his shoulder in her driveway.

"Good evening, Madam. Mr. Beauchamp is awaiting your arrival" said the limo driver.

"Limousine? That man is out of his mind" Gigi whispered under her breath.

She hated limousines. Well she didn't actually hate limousines, she hated people who tried to impress her with them. Hired cars *never* impressed her. Anyone with $250 and a debit card could rent a limo for a few hours but a man who *owned* the limousine company...now that would be impressive.

"Tell Mr. Beauchamp thank you but I won't be needing his car. I'll be driving myself on this evening but tell him thank you and that I appreciate the gesture" she said and closed the door.

Did he really think this was a date and how did that car get past the security gate she wondered? Security should have called her and gotten her okay before allowing him up to her house.

She sent the limo away, hopped into her own BMW X5 and drove to Hyde Park Grille in Woodmere Village for her meeting with the infamous Evan Beauchamp. The rumor mill was constantly a chatter concerning him and his womanizing. Stories flourished about the many bricks that had been thrown through his windows or the numerous times his different cars had been keyed. She worked too long and too hard to earn a good name for herself and refused to have it ruined by associating with a drama king like him in a romantic manner.

She stopped at the gas station less than one mile from her destination to satisfy a sudden urge for chewing gum and laughed aloud at herself. Why was she behaving like a teenager and playing this game with a man she didn't care about and wasn't the least bit interested in?

Finally, she arrived at her destination thirty minutes past the appointed time and she *still* got there before Evan did even with her pit stop.

"Ms. Haralson" the hostess approached her, "Mr. Beauchamp has a car waiting to take you to a different location for your engagement tonight."

She didn't have time to play games with this man all night and he was making her very angry. Either he was going to agree to join the Tour or not, sans all the dramatics. She felt like she was in the middle of a spy suspense thriller with all the foolish secrecy.

She chewed her bottom lip which she often did when she was nervous or angry or both and reluctantly agreed to join Evan in his car. She smiled nervously at the hostess as she escorted her to the limo where the driver she'd dismissed earlier in the evening held the car door open. He smiled sheepishly and displayed his pleasure with watching Gigi play a game they both knew had a deck heavily stacked against her.

The driver opened the door and there was the infamous Evan Beauchamp smiling like a Cheshire cat. His teeth were straight and white complimented by skin reminiscent of the amber tones in honey and seemed flawless under the moon shining in from the roof. He wore a simple white t-shirt, a pair of jeans and a black jacket that perfectly framed his broad shoulders. A pair of all white Nike Air Force One sneakers adorned his feet and a single, Emerald cut, 2-carat diamond solitaire embellished the left ear of the gorgeous man. She now understood why women lost their damn minds over him.

"Hello Ms. Haralson" he said as she slid into the open door of the limousine.

Her name rolled off his tongue like silk. She didn't like smooth operators like him at all and she was uneasy. She didn't know what it was but something didn't feel right and she wanted to complete her business and leave his company as quickly as possible.

The bar was stocked with Moet & Chandon Imperial Rose which was one of her favorites. It was a fluke for sure that he just happened to have her favorite champagne she assured herself. There's no way he could have known that but he was smooth, she had to give him that.

"Hello Mr. Beauchamp. Finally, we can sit down and talk about the Tour" Gigi said in her stern, best, business-like voice.

"Glass Slipper Media has made Black Ice an offer you can't possibly consider refusing. No, you won't be headlining this time but it's an awesome deal nonetheless."

The group's attorney and manager had already reviewed the figures and advised the group to accept the contract terms. They were supposed to be in her office at nine the next morning but nobody bothered to tell Gigi, the Director or Talent Procurement that.

She was far more beautiful than he thought she would be and he was mesmerized by her brown eyes. She found herself staring at his mouth as he spoke and watched his lips form words in syncopation with his tongue. She allowed her mind to question what he did at night with that tongue and she felt her nipples stiffen. He was a notorious ladies man but she still found herself being drawn in by his magnetism and overt sexuality.

"The most beautiful garment a woman can wear is her smile and you wear it beautifully" Evan flirted.

"May I offer you a glass of Champagne" he asked and eyed her seductively. He poured her a glass and offered it to her.

"I'm sorry Mr. Beauchamp, I never drink while I am working" she protested.

"Okay, I can respect that" he answered. "So, Al Bernard and I plan to drop in at GSM early tomorrow morning and put our John Hancock on that contract. I ain't been on tour in a minute" he said and ran his hand down his goatee. I ain't hung out with some of those cats for what, ten years, maybe more. That shit was wild back in the day" he grinned deviously. "Now, that should take care of business and you're officially off the clock. Now, about that champagne…"

"I really don't think that would be a good idea" she tried to say but he was all over her before she could get all of the words out. He cupped her face in his hands and suddenly kissed her. Gigi slapped his face hard enough to draw tears and shoved him off of her.

"Punk, who the hell do you think you are" she snapped. "Put your gotdamn hands on me again and see what the hell happens! Stop this got damn car before I wind up fucking you the fuck up! Let me out this motherfucker!"

How dare Evan invade her space and touch her without permission. He's lucky she hadn't sprayed mace in his face whether he was a fine, superstar millionaire or not.

"Anjelica, I'm so sorry, I didn't mean to offend you. I was out of line and I apologize but you're so beautiful, I just wanted to kiss you, that's all. I'll have my driver return you to your car at once."

"Your driver don't need to take me no damn where" she screamed at Evan. "I'll get to my car on my own!"

Gigi bolted out of the limousine and stormed across the parking lot to the main street. She hated haughty, overconfident, vain, self-absorbed and proud men like him and he had a lot of nerve putting his hands on her. The imposition was not appreciated.

She reached for her clutch to pull out her car keys and realized she left them both in the limo. She was disgusted that she had to go back into the lion's den but she needed her clutch. She turned to go back and landed right in Evan's arms. She shoved him away as he tried to apologize and explain himself further but she wasn't trying to hear it, she was furious.

Her eyes were drawn to his baby soft lips that were perfectly shaped and made to suck a woman's bottom lip or her labia or both. His teeth sparkled like freshly fallen snow on a crisp, moonlit winter night and had distracted her while those wildly sensuous lips transgressed against her.

He would never get the chance to violate her again if she had anything to do with it. *He* was a dangerous man and she was determined to stay out of his path yet in the back of her mind, she knew she hadn't seen the last of Evan Beauchamp.

Chapter 2

Under His Aegis

Oshen Benjamin mumbled to himself as he changed the station on the radio. The airwaves were clogged with songs about big booties and vulgar sex acts and it turned him off.

The hip-hop genre had evolved into a sex-driven, polyamorous, misogynistic culture that objectified women and Oshen wasn't on it. He believed every man only needed one woman and he should focus on giving his all to her rather than parts and pieces to many.

Oshen was a franchise player for the Cleveland Lightening professional football organization and their whole run game had been designed around him.

The football gods took one part Marcus Allen, one-part Earl Campbell, added some Marshawn Lynch and a dash of Lesean McCoy to create the supernova running back that was Oshen Benjamin. His wealth and influence gave him access to a diverse plethora of women but they were not women of quality. They were beautiful but only interested in his money, prestige and notoriety. It seemed like no one wanted to get to know him for who he was so he remained single and unattached.

He searched through radio stations and found nothing to his liking then turned the radio off. He connected his smartphone to the auxiliary cord and opted to listen to his playlist instead.

He liked old school hip-hop but he enjoyed old-school R&B even more and settled on an old Ralph Tresvant album entitled 'Sensitivity'.

"You need a man, with sen-si-ti-vity, a man like me" he sang out loud along with the lead singer of the R&B boy group New Edition.

'The Sensitivity' album was his favorite of the solo efforts of New Edition alum. Bobby Brown had the most commercial success but Johnny Gill's self-titled album and BBD's (Bell, Biv, and Devoe) 'Poison' didn't perform too shabbily on the record charts either. 'Sensitivity' just happened to be his favorite.

He had no particular destination tonight. He decided earlier in the day that it would be the perfect night to break in his brand new truck. The moon was high, the stars were bright and the roads were clear so he cruised the city streets and people watched.

Wintertime was an amazing time to do that with folk scurrying to and fro' all bundled up and waddling like penguins. Only their eyes peaked out from between the layers of scarves, hats, mittens and gloves. Fashion was a thing of summer's past in northeast Ohio and it was far too cold to be cute…except her.

He sat at the light as it cycled from red to green to yellow and red again ignoring the motorists angrily honking behind him. Her crème colored cashmere coat was perfectly paired with crème gloves and boots which exquisitely complimented her calves and was mesmerized by her beauty.

She was moving very quickly across the parking lot at Zion's with a man in hot pursuit. He wanted to jump out of his truck and run to rescue her, being the chivalrous man that he was, but experience taught him to wait first and thoroughly assess the situation. The last thing he needed was to insert himself into a condition where both of the parties involved turned around and attacked him. He looked a little longer at the woman and realized he knew her: it was Gigi Haralson.

"Gigi" Oshen yelled across the street, "are you okay? Do you need help?"

That was against his better judgment.

Gigi was stunning but the girl was extra. He was introduced to her at a function for his team hosted by Glass Slipper Media maybe three or four months prior. They had a few things in common and he found her intriguing enough to ask her out.

They enjoyed dinner together a couple of times so he wasn't sure why she never called him after the third date. That confused him a bit because he thought they connected and had a good time. Even with all of the extra, he would have taken her out again in a minute so it didn't really matter why she never called him again.

A woman like her was rare in his circles because the women he normally encountered bored him to tears. All they brought to the table was a pretty face and a round behind and those kinds of women were under the false impression that was all they *needed* to bring to the table. Fine and dumb might have worked with other men but that would never be the key that unlocked his heart. There had to be substance behind the pretty. *She* was funny, beautiful *and* smart. It was the God thing that got on his nerves. *That* was the extra.

Why didn't he just keep going? The Lightening's bye week was this Sunday and Oshen wanted to enjoy his off time. He was trying to chill tonight but now he's in the middle of someone else's drama. He should have gone home and surprised his mother.

Women and girls had coddled and catered to Oshen since he was seven years old. His promise as an athlete was evident early and *everyone* around him worshipped him for as long as he could remember. Even now, he had an entire half-billion-dollar operation dancing to his beat but Gigi Haralson wouldn't lay on her back for him. She wouldn't even kiss him.

She was the first and only woman to ever rebuff his advances, talking some nonsense about waiting for God and not confusing good sex with love. That made his dick hard and he simply couldn't resist making a new play for her.

He was from Beggs, Oklahoma which was a teeny tiny town in central Oklahoma, right outside of Tulsa and country as hell. It boasted a population of less than 1,000 people and a geographic area of less than 5 square miles. The median income was about $31,000 per year which meant the town was poor as hell too.

He tried his best to get his mother to move but she refused. She loved it in Beggs. She said she liked the down home feel and would never trade it for the likes of a big city. She much preferred swinging in her porch swing with a tall glass of fresh lemonade and a good book on lazy summer afternoons. She wouldn't leave her beloved homestead for anything in the world.

Now his father was a different story all together. He was sick and tired of herding cattle, shucking corn, shelling pecans and picking cotton. He would have liked nothing more than to move to Florida, play golf and drink beer for the rest of his life, on Oshen's dime, of course.

He cut across several lanes of traffic and pulled into Zion's parking lot. He squinted his eyes in the dark to verify the man pursuing Gigi was who he thought it was. It was Evan Beauchamp and he hated that weasel.

During, Oshen's rookie year, he received a phone call from his high school sweetheart while at training camp informing him that she was pregnant and *keeping* the baby. He was excited about being a husband and father and bought her the largest, clearest pear shaped diamond ring he could afford on his league minimum salary and asked her to marry him. So many people were giving birth to children without benefit of marriage and that was troublesome to Oshen. He had been raised with both parents in the home and wanted the same solid, nuclear structure for his children.

What he didn't know was his girl was not only cheating with that asshole but was carrying *his* baby not Oshen's. It took a DNA test to reveal the truth that he was not the father once her cheating finally broke them up. and he hadn't been the same since.

"Oshen! Thank God!" Gigi let out a long, exhausted sigh and continued. "Will you tell this punk to get his hands off of me and give me my clutch before I call the police on him?"

"Drama," he thought to himself as Evan walked towards his truck with an outstretched hand.

He jumped out and brushed past Evan to help Gigi climb into the passenger seat. He chuckled as he watched her lumber up into his huge pick-up and try to be coy at the same time. He scooped her up into his arms and gently placed her onto the seat. He fastened her seatbelt into place and turned his attention to the rat.

"Yo, E, the lady needs her bag" Oshen bellowed into the night air as he walked over to where Evan stood.

Evan Beauchamp had never watched another man walk away with his girl in his whole life and it wasn't about to happen tonight either. Oshen Benjamin was not going to drive off into the night with *his* date and if by some fluke he did, he wanted his money back for the limousine.

He was wildly handsome with movie star good looks and a lot of money. There was nothing nor anyone for that matter that he couldn't buy or sell. Everybody had a price, it was simply a matter of figuring out what it was.

The two of them couldn't stand one another. Oshen blamed him for the situation with Mayven and the baby. It wasn't Evan's fault Oshen left his girl to go chase footballs.

In fact, it was *his* fault the whole thing ever even happened. If Oshen hadn't left her alone while he was with the Carolina Tigers, she wouldn't have been at the club that night and had she never gone to the club that night she would have never ran into Evan and his entourage, Evan would never have been able to choose her and they would have never snuck around behind Oshen's back for all those months. She then doesn't get pregnant, doesn't lie to Oshen, and they don't break his little heart.

That's *that* man's bad. He never should have left his chic alone. Evan walked back to the limousine and grabbed Gigi's clutch.

"Give my regards to the lady." Evan said.

"Whatever" responded Oshen nonchalantly as he walked back to his truck. He grinned to himself and drove off with Gigi sitting comfortably beside him.

"Have you eaten, my Lady?" he asked her, "Want to grab a quick bite?"

She was famished but she still didn't want to be seen in the presence of *the* Oshen Benjamin. He was fine, wealthy, engaging, witty, funny and captivating but the ladies threw themselves at him. They could care less whether or not he was with her. She saw them request he sign autographs on their breasts, wrote their phone numbers down on panties, and dropped room keys and house keys in his drink. Three dates with him and that madness had been enough for her.

They laid at his feet and that was drama she had no desire to be a part of.

She was hungry though and agreed to go to dinner with him. It wasn't a date she simplified. She wasn't trying to marry the man and he wasn't trying to marry her. They were just two hungry people going to eat. She would even pay her own check.

Gigi wanted a good old fashioned hamburger with cheese and grilled onions, mushrooms and green peppers. The kind where the grease runs down your hand when you bite into it and the mustard, ketchup and mayo gather in the corners of your mouth. Yes. She wanted one of those fat, greasy homemade mommy burgers with some fresh cut fries and a little malt vinegar. She craved a fresh hand dipped strawberry milkshake, too. She could taste it already. She would definitely hug the toilet in the morning, though, no doubt about it.

"Oshen, would you mind if we went to this quiet little bar in Solon? They have the best burgers."

"If the lady wants a burger, the lady gets a burger. Where to?

Chapter 3

Chance Encounters

Gigi sat across from Oshen and listened to him talk. She never realized how intelligent he truly was. She previously dismissed him as *just* your stereotypical athlete: all brawn, no brain. She found it refreshing to hear him speak about sales projections and marketing strategies pertaining to a new product he recently introduced to the marketplace.

He had a Bachelor's Degree in Business Administration from Oklahoma University and was studying to earn his M.B.A. This man was more than fine and she was quietly impressed.

She liked *this* Oshen, she liked him a lot. They talked so much that her mouth and her throat was dry. She was comfortable with him like an old grade school friend. She had revealed a lot about herself to him without realizing it. In the short span of a few hours, he had become her friend.

She excused herself from the table to "powder her nose" and ventured off to wash her hands in the bathroom before dinner.

She carried a bottle of sanitizer in her purse, every woman does, but she preferred to wash her hands with soap and water and get what she considered a cleaner clean. She pulled her phone from her bag to check her messages and ran smack dab into a brick wall. Gigi fell to the floor and cried out in pain.

She'd twisted her ankle and instantly regretted wearing her damn Louis boots. That would have never happened in her cute, sequined boots she wore with jeans or leggings.

She felt herself being lifted to her feet by the gentleman she'd run headlong into who'd bent down to help her.

"Here, let me help you. Are you okay?" he asked.

"My ankle hurts just a little but I'll be okay." said Gigi as she winced in pain.

"I'm so sorry, I didn't see you. I was engrossed in my text messages". She finally looked up at the stranger and gasped loudly. It was Chance.

"Chance, is that you? Now what are the odds of me seeing you here? Oh my goodness" she gushed.

"This is one of my favorite places" he responded excitedly, "I'm here all the time. I brought you here, don't you remember?"

She didn't remember but she *did* remember the way he set her body on fire with his enchanted tongue a few hours ago. She grinned at the way he always smacked her ass when he kissed it and the way his tongue felt in between her cheeks. She loved the way his dick danced on her tonsils when she swallowed it and choked on it. She loved it when he reached over her elongated body to make her ass bounce and fucked her pussy with his fingers while she sucked him off and she yearned for the way he felt when he entered her from behind and the pain and pleasure she derived from his too big penis.

"Gigi? Seriously, are you okay? Can I call someone to take you home and make you forget you're hurting" he asked and moved in close.

His voice brought her back to reality and she shook her head a few times to clear the very recent memories.

He was concerned about her ankle being worse than she led on and crinkled his brow at her.

"No" she replied "I'm okay. Besides I'm here with a friend. He'll help me if I need it, I'm not by myself" she said.

"I saw that" Chance answered, "Isn't that Oshen Benjamin I saw you out there with? You still working? You didn't have time for me earlier because you said you were meeting Evan Beauchamp. That don't look like him to me that looks like Oshen Benjamin" he said while nodding his head in Oshen's direction.

"Yes, that's him but we're just friends and I really did have to work tonight, I promise you. It's a long, long story but I did meet with Evan earlier. Anyway, I'll see you a little later I hope" she said.

She was still very much attracted to him and still wanted to enjoy that late night tryst with him later. She didn't want him to walk away believing she and Oshen were an item.

"Okay, well if everything is good with you, I'm going to head home. Killer Wave is on his way and I don't want that problem. Besides, a brother has to work tomorrow."

One of the wait staff had gone to inform Oshen of her mishap and he was making his way towards her.

"I understand that because a sister does too and by the way, you won't have a problem with Killer Wave. Like I said, we're just friends. He is *not* my man" she said. "Goodnight."

Her heart felt guilty because she had broken his. He was a rebound relationship that neither one of them should have been in so soon after their mutual divorces. It wasn't love, it was sex but he couldn't separate the two. He was crushed when she broke it off then and the look on his face told her he was crushed now that she was with someone else now.

She watched Chance and Oshen exchange pleasantries as he made his way back to his table. She guessed it was safe to assume the freak-fest for tonight was cancelled and *that* was a bummer.

"Who was that" Oshen asked as he approached.

"Oh nobody, just a guy I used to deal with a little while back, no big deal and I'm fine by the way.

"So what, you've been fucking him and just happen to literally run into him tonight? That's bullshit. Are you sure you didn't call him to ride shotgun?"

"Nope, it's just coincidence that's all and I am *not* fucking him, thank you very much" she lied and looked over his shoulder.

"Great! They're bringing our burgers. Let's go eat. I'm starved."

"They're bringing *your* burger and *my* grilled salmon. I can't stay in *this* kind of shape eating greasy burgers and fries."

"And *I* can't maintain my plus size figure eating nasty ass fish. I hate seafood, ick" she said jokingly and leaned on him and limped back to the table.

He watched her as she dug into her food. She didn't eat cute like the rest of his dates who normally pushed their little dainty salads around on their plate, nibbling a piece of lettuce or a carrot every now again. She wasn't like that. Sure, she cut the burger into smaller, more manageable pieces but she enjoyed her food. She would cover her mouth when chewing which was to be expected but she actually ate.

He was enjoying himself and wanted to spend more time with her outside of tonight even though he thought it a bit strange that she runs into one of her exes and now said ex watched her every move from across the room. He was convinced she set the whole thing up because that's how women are and that's what women do. Still, he contemplated asking her for another date, a real date this time.

Oshen and Gigi talked into the wee hours of the morning, shutting the little local bar down. He finally drove her back to her car at closing time wondering exactly who she was. She wasn't the same woman he went out with a few months ago. She wasn't so uptight, so guarded. She was calm and unsuspicious, healed. Well, maybe not healed but scabbed over for sure.

He wondered if that was due to that guy back at the restaurant hitting her with his log on a regular basis. She denied that they were still sleeping together but the way he looked at her said otherwise. There was just something about that guy he didn't like. He couldn't put his finger on it but there was just something.

He took her back to where she parked her truck and followed her home. He debated with himself the entire way if he should kiss her goodnight. She slapped fire out of Evan when he tried. Would she slap him too if he did? He wondered if she would cuss him out, pretend to be mad and then invite him in and sleep with him like the rest of these broads out here, or would she play shy, bid him adieu and graciously close the door in his face. He decided to put the kiss on the back burner but he was certainly going to ask her for an actual date.

His heart sank as they pulled into the driveway of her condo. There it sat, glistening under the moonlight. There was a box of long stemmed roses, at least a dozen, maybe more. with a big red bow. He sent those kinds of boxes more times than he could think of so he knew what they looked like at first glance.

"Looks like you have some brother's nose open wide" he remarked to her as he helped her along the winding walk to the front door. He would have bet money they were from the man at the bar.

"Oshen, I'm not seeing anyone. I have no clue who those are from" she lied.

Chance was still warming her bed regularly and would be doing so right now had he not seen them tonight but he didn't need to know that.

She wondered how people continued to get to her condo through the guarded front gate. She lived in a gated community for a reason. The limo driver, Chance and now this was unacceptable. She appreciated the gesture whoever they were from but she was unhappy about people having easy access to her house. She would address it in the morning.

He stooped down to grab the box while she fumbled with her keys and pleasantly found himself eye-to-eye with the most beautiful ass he'd ever seen. It wasn't big and ignorant but round and firm like a Red Delicious apple and he found himself wanting to take a big, juicy bite.

He was distracted from staring at her bottom by the box he held in his hands. He thought, no he was *sure* there was something alive in the box, thrashing about, trying to gain its freedom.

"Um, Beautiful" Oshen said, "something in this damn box is *moving!*"

He lifted the box over his head and threw it across the lawn like the Greek god Zeus hurling a lightning bolt through the air. It floated in slow motion and roses and baby's breath made their way out of the box and strewn across the grass, finally landing in the middle of the quiet street with a thud.

"What the fuck" he whispered and squinted to get a clearer view.

She stood next to him with her mouth opened wide and was also stunned as they were riveted by the sight of dozens of snakes slithering in the street that two minutes ago were in the flower box. They groveled and crawled onto lawns, under bushes and into sewers and several of them seemed to be sliding directly towards the couple.

"Baby?! Unlock the damn door" Oshen cried.

He did *not* mess with snakes. There was nothing he hated more than a snake. He'd been bitten by one as a young boy at his uncle's farm in North Carolina and although it had been non-venomous the event still traumatized him.

Gigi finally got the front door unlocked and they both stumbled into the foyer of the beautiful two story condo and quickly slammed the door behind them.

"Hell to the motherfucking no" yelled Oshen, "You need to turn on some damn lights in here, Anjelica!!!"

She turned on the lamp on the table with trembling hands and weak, unsteady knees. The light in the foyer didn't alleviate any of the stress caused by the snakes as it illuminated tens of dozens of additional black roses. The floor was covered with them. This kind of stuff only happened in the movies or on TV not to real people.

"Fuck that, let's go" he told her and grabbed her hand.

She chewed her bottom lip and didn't move.

"There's no discussion, Anjelica. You will *not* be staying here tonight so let's go and don't say shit about it."

He pulled her by the hand and reached for the door.

"But Oshen…" she protested and pulled her hand away and limped away from him.

He was having none of her irrational objections. Black roses were inside the house and they'd just escaped snakes slithering around on the outside of the house. He refused to argue with her regarding the issue and the matter was not up for debate.

He gathered her up into his arms and carried her kicking and screaming to his truck, got them both securely into their seatbelts and sped away faster than a driver on the NASCAR circuit.

His mind was spinning. He never in his 32 years of life saw anything like that. It was as if he were watching a movie starring the two of them but this was real.

He glanced over at the visibly shaken Gigi with her disheveled hair and smeared makeup and found this fragile, frightened creature to be more beautiful than she'd ever been to him before. She was imperfectly perfect for him and he decided in that moment that he was going to marry her.

"Baby, what the fuck was that all about" he asked. "You must have that good shit to make a brother flip like that, seriously, man. Like for real."

"Oshen, I told you before, I swear to you I don't have men on me all like that" she sighed and continued to lie to him. "I have no idea who could have done that or even why, I promise you."

"Well, you're not staying in *that* house tonight or any other night if I have anything to say about it" he replied. "I know I'm not your man, not yet anyways but my place is huge and there's more than enough space for the both of us. You're more than welcome to stay as long as you'd like"

"Oshen no, that is *not* going to happen. Please take me to a hotel. I'm a pretty big girl, I can take care of myself."

He pulled into the nearest parking lot and put the car in park.

"Look, someone, you claim not to know who, has gone into your house and took their time to set up something intricate like that and for some reason, you think you're a big girl and can take care of yourself, huh?" he continued "That's some bull *and* some shit together right there so unless you have a pistol up in there somewhere and a dog bigger than that little rat here's how this is going down: Your sexy ass *will* be staying with me, I don't give half a damn if that's agreeable to you or not, that's what the fuck it is. We'll make a police report in the morning and I'll get you a bodyguard tomorrow as well so until that happens there is no going into downtown Cleveland for you. What size do you wear? I'm thinking a fourteen maybe sixteen, am I right? Anyway, I'll call my stylist to bring you some things over for tonight and tomorrow until she can shop for you."

"Oshen, I appreciate the gesture, I really do" she said. "I *love* the fact that you want to protect me, what women wouldn't but I will not be forced out of my own home and I *can* take care of myself, thank you" Gigi pouted.

She was shocked and couldn't believe he had spoken to her like that. People who talked to her like that didn't have a job anymore and normally ended up on the unemployment line.

He shook his head at her objection and put the truck in gear to pull out of the parking lot.

"Girl, shut that stupid shit up!"

That same night

Sydney Zanchak-Taylor twirled her long red locks around her index finger. She had been trying to reach Gigi for hours. She worried about her friend especially since she had been out with the infamous Evan Beauchamp.

"That bitch better have a good motherfucking reason for not answering the phone" she said aloud.

"Man, fuck that whore" her husband shouted. "Get your ass over here and handle your shit."

Here she was calling Gigi when she should have been concentrating on Tim and taking care of her man.

Sydney's husband, Tim Taylor, knew how to please her. He knew exactly where to place his tongue and precisely how long to manipulate her before she dripped her crisis all over his face. There were a few times when it seemed like her thighs would crack his head like a nut but she always loosened her grip on him right before he passed out.

She thought about those nutcrackers that were popular around Christmas-time and the way they just about smashed the nut into nut paste. That was specifically how much pressure she applied to his head when he was sucking her clit and she was about to explode.

Sydney's mouth ran incessantly. She was more than a handful; she was a straight up pistol. The girl couldn't cook worth a damn and she half cleaned ever since the kids reached adulthood. She didn't do much of anything except work and screw…and run up behind that damn Gigi.

"Why you always in that girl's business" Tim questioned. "That's a grown ass woman fucking with a grown ass man. She knows what's up." He hated Gigi.

Sydney was sitting at her vanity table with her back to him. She looked at his reflection in the vanity mirror and could see that he was becoming agitated, irritated and even angry. He was spoiled and didn't like to share her attention with their kids, their grandkids, her momma, the dog, nobody.

"That's my girl" she answered, and you know damn well if there's a loser within a two-hundred-mile radius he's going to be drawn to her. Somebody got to have her back."

Tim nodded his head in agreement because Sydney was right. He really didn't like Gigi but he had to admit that she was smart, pretty and really did have it together. She made her own money, had her own house and was the total package but the woman couldn't find a decent man for nothing in the world.

"Why is she not answering" Sydney whispered, confused.

Every time her friend didn't respond the more worried she became. It was out of the ordinary for Gigi not to answer a call from Sydney. She may have let calls from other people go to voicemail on her personal cell but she always answered calls from Sydney.

She left another voicemail message then called the bum Evan. She had dinner with him tonight and if anybody knew where she was, it'd be that dude.

"Get your ass over here and take care of your man. I'm fucking hungry. Get over here and feed me and let me suck that pussy."

She hung up the phone and hightailed it over to where he lay. He sat up and placed tiny light kisses all over her belly then spun her around and nibbled at her ass cheeks while his free hand rolled her clit. He turned her back around so he could lick her and slipped his fingers into her asshole. She was a freak like that. She loved anal and he was preparing her ass to receive him.

He placed her hand on her pussy and leaned back so he could watch her play with herself. He enjoyed sitting back and watching her manipulate her own body, fondle her own breasts and offer him her erect nipples after she's sucked them to ridged peaks. She was an amazing sexual being and when he watched her bring herself to her own summit, he was hard enough to break bricks.

He was an incredibly over-sexed man. He'd been with Sydney twenty years and married to her for seventeen of them yet she was clueless as to how deep his sexual well went. If he had anything to do with it, she would soon fine out.

He laid her out with her legs spread wide on the bed and knelt by the bedside, handcuffs in hand. There would be no backing across the bed tonight.

"She is going to love this pussy right here", he thought to himself as he sat back and admired his wife.

Sydney had a beautiful vaginal area. It wasn't naked but she kept it trimmed perfectly. He asked her for a threesome before but she hadn't been interested in the idea of being with another woman. He always entertained fantasies of another woman eating his wife's pussy while he stuffed her with his thick dick. It was most definitely going to go down but he still needed a little time to open her up to the concept.

The sound of Sydney's ringing cell phone breached the thick sexual air. She knew it was Gigi, pushed Tim away, jumped up and ran to answer it.

"You all right?"

Her voice was simultaneously worried, relieved and annoyed. She twisted her hair around her finger and engrossed herself so deeply in the details of Gigi's evening that she never saw Tim dress and leave.

He was outraged that she had again placed Gigi higher than him on her "To Do" list. All day long, he was riveted by the thought of her, how she'd move, what she'd say, all of the things he'd do to her. To be pushed away and rejected by his own wife in favor of her girl was crossing the line and he wondered if they were sexing each other. He couldn't think of another explanation why a woman would do such a thing.

Tim pulled into the driveway and sat there for a moment as he did each time he found himself at Dionne's place. He always reasoned with himself and his conscience for this particular side piece. There was no doubt he loved his wife but he had physical needs she hadn't been meeting lately and he had to do what he had to do.

He and Dionne had been involved for a little more than a year now since he met her picking Sydney up from work one day. He felt a little remorse when he discovered she was his wife's co-worker but Sydney had been slipping and Tim needed a piece of pussy like he needed air.

He reached under his front passenger seat and pulled out a box of condoms. He always laced up especially with this one. He was a cheater but it wasn't worth taking a disease or a baby home to his wife.

He started towards the front door to ring the doorbell and at the last minute remembered he had his own key. He let himself in the back door and there she was in the kitchen, wearing nothing but a smile.

"Damn girl! What the fuck is up" asked Tim.

"Bring that dick over here and find the fuck out" said Dionne and dropped to her knees.

Chapter 4

Love at First Sight

Wednesday November 5, 2014

A huge smile crossed Gigi's face as she was awakened by the wafting smell of bacon in the air. She stretched and shifted her body in a strange bed and panic set in. She surveyed her surroundings and wondered where she was, then breathed a sigh of relief when she remembered she was at Oshen's.

He'd surprised her last night and let her see his sensitive side, his normal side not the superstar that everyone else sees. He showed her the part of him that she could fall in love with but then again, he *was* Oshen Benjamin. How many women have thought that before?

Gigi knelt to pray as she always did. She knew she wasn't perfect and a lot of times flat out wrong with the situations she got herself into but even in her imperfection, she loved the Lord. Her relationship with Jesus Christ was real and personal and she was nothing without it.

After she prayed, she leapt out of bed and rushed to get dressed. It was 11:00 a.m. and she was crazy late for work. She remembered Oshen said something about her not going to work today and she literally laughed out loud. He wasn't her Daddy, husband or her man and couldn't tell her what to do. In fact, nobody told Gigi Haralson what to do.

"Good morning, Beautiful" Oshen said.

She spun around and gulped. A wave of relief rushed over her to see it was him especially with the foolishness of last night fresh on her mind.

"How about breakfast" Oshen asked. She had to get to work and soon. She didn't want to get behind in her work because she would never catch up.

"Thanks Oshen but I've got to go to work" she declined.

"Nope, not happening. I told you that last night. First, you're going to have a good breakfast, after that you're going to go to the closet and grab an outfit my stylist put together for you and then, we're going to file that police report" answered Oshen. Gigi wasn't happy with him telling her what to do but he was right and she reluctantly agreed.

"Okay" she said "not because you said so but because it's logical and it makes sense. Where are your bath towels?"

He smiled and shook his head at this intelligent, witty, funny, sweet, giving, honest, and absolutely gorgeous spit fire.

He'd analyzed her last night and came to the conclusion that she could actually be the one woman who could fit flawlessly into his life and compliment him in a way no one else could. He wanted to get to know the ugly side of her, the raw, naked underbelly of who she was. He wanted her.

He left the breakfast tray on her bedside table and went to his office. One of the first things to be addressed this morning was to list her condo for sale. There had been a security breach and she wasn't safe there. He called Brenda Welch, rumored to be the top broker of high end real estate in Northeast Ohio and set the appointment for one o'clock after they filed the police report. He hung up the phone and looked up to find her standing in the doorway, staring at him disapprovingly.

"Exactly who do you think you are" she yelled, "and who the hell gave you permission to sell anything of mine?"

She was wearing the beautiful satin robe he purchased for her earlier that morning. He told her his stylist brought over some things for her but the truth was he shopped for her himself. An acquaintance owned a small upscale boutique at Eton Square and she opened it at 8:00 a.m. as a favor to him. He chose each piece himself and in his opinion he did an awesome job. The robe hugged every curve of her body just as he imagined it would.

"What you talking about, Girl" he asked and hurriedly brushed past her. His dick had gotten hard at the sight of her. He didn't want her to see it and get the wrong impression. He wanted her but not in the middle of this and not right now.

"Oshen, do not walk away from me" she yelled. "You know exactly what the hell I'm talking about, Boy! I'm a grown ass woman! Who the hell you calling Girl?!"

"I'm talking to your little short ass right now damn it" he whirled around and yelled back, "ain't no damn body else here! Quit acting like a whiny ass baby and face fucking facts!! You cannot, as a matter of fact, you will not stay at your place ever again. The shit ain't safe and you already know that bullshit, quit fucking playing! Now get dressed and let's go!!"

She was furious. She'd spent the last twelve of the previous thirteen years of her life being controlled, manipulated, berated, demeaned, screamed at, yelled at and abused. She vowed to herself to never allow that to happen again. She didn't care who he was he would not talk to her like that.

"First of all" she said, "I don't know who you thought I was but let's get you some fucking understanding, I am *not* the one you want to try like that. Number two, you don't run a single thing when it comes to me do you understand that, not a single, solitary, got damn thing. You don't talk to nobody about nothing to do with me unless you talk to me first and I ain't selling my damn house! You understand that shit? Do you understand English? What you speaking, French? Well, que comprenez-vous? Or do you prefer Spanish? Entiende que motherfucker?"

He stood silently as he glowered down upon her. Stares, glares like that from her ex-husband preacher were normally followed by a slap or a choke and an intense fear gripped Gigi's heart. She knew what the danger zone looked and sounded like and she was in it. She could hear the sound of her own heart beating deafeningly loud.

"Are you finished with your little tantrum" he asked and moved closer to her.

"Excuse me, you're in my space" she answered and quickly walked down the hall to the guest room and slammed the door.

He stood silently and listened to her once commanding voice quiver when she spoke. She was afraid of him and he wondered who had placed that kind of fear in her heart.

He lightly knocked on the bedroom door and called her name. He had to think of a way to make her feel comfortable, in control and eliminate any real or perceived distress she may have felt.

She opened the door to find him on his knees, allowing her to tower over him.

"Let's talk" he said but she slammed the door and retreated back into the bedroom. He stood and leaned against the door.

"I promise you don't have to fear me" he said through the closed door "and I would never harm you, ever. I'm not that kind of guy."

There was still no response from the other side of the closed door.

"Gigi okay, I'm sorry, I should have never called Brenda without asking you first and I promise not to ever take control of your life again, okay? Now will you open the door so we can talk?"

She slowly opened the door and he rushed in, grabbed her and kissed her. His tongue twirled with hers and he flitted the tip of his across the tip of hers. Her initial resistance gave way to a deep, ardent response and their tongues danced an erotic dance for what seemed like hours. They broke the kiss and stared into each other's eyes, each searching for permission from the other to continue.

He drew her closer to him and kissed her some more. What was she thinking? Outside of a few dates, this man was a stranger to her. Besides that, she was definitely still riding

Chance's dick on the regular so what kind of woman would allow herself to be in intimate situations like this with two men at one time?

His kiss had her body reacting in ways Chance never came close to causing and all of her reasoning went flying out of the window He was igniting a lust in her she never knew existed and she couldn't, or wouldn't fight it.

Oshen pressed his weight against her pinning her to the wall. She must really be the one, he rationalized as he had never brought a woman to his house before. That had been his unwritten rule. He always went to their place, that way no drama visited his front door. None of the casual women knew where he lived but Gigi was no causal woman.

He fell in love with her last night and although she didn't know it yet, she was *his* woman. He suspected she was still doing that dude back at the restaurant but he planned to keep her so satisfied she wouldn't have the time or the energy to entertain him. He was going to make it his business to have her climbing every wall in every room of his house.

He laid her on the floor and lowered himself down to lay beside her. She was trembling either from fear or anticipation, he wasn't sure which.

He could tell she'd been deeply hurt and didn't want her to feel that ever again especially not by his hand. He also gathered from her conversation, her declaration of being independent and constantly repeating the fact that she could take care of herself that she'd been disappointed a number of times and refused to depend on another man and let it happen again. He didn't want to be just another man who disenchanted her, who let her down.

That's why he wanted her. He could tell she didn't want to be just another one of many to a man but *his* only one. Everything else was just a smoke screen.

He believed her when she said the man at the restaurant was her ex but he didn't believe a word she said about not still being in a physical situation-ship with him. He wanted to love her and when he looked into her eyes a second time, he understood that she knew that.

He hungrily discovered her mouth with his tongue. He'd never believed in love at first sight before but the way he devoured her and the way she silently invited him to do so confirmed to him that this was it. He ran his fingers through her shoulder length hair and turned her head to expose her neck He zealously kissed it and nibbled it leaving passion marks in his stead like a teenager.

He groped around blindly under her robe, fiddling with the sash before he finally found her large, hard nipples. They were shaped like his favorite red, sugar coated gumdrop sand he licked and suckled them tenderly as she whimpered beneath his touch.

Her tits were quite pretty and tasted amazing, especially for a woman 13 years his senior but those luscious nipples were not the treasure he sought this morning. This wasn't about him and what he wanted, it was all about giving her the pleasure she so obviously needed and had been denied. He was sure old dude back at the restaurant was fucking her on the regular but he wasn't touching her in her soul. Her eyes told him that.

He sat up and faced her then grabbed Gigi by her legs and pulled her towards him. He untied the sash of her robe to expose her ample body which she immediately tried to cover, murmuring something about being too fat. She was incredibly sexy and he wanted her, he didn't care if she weighed 125 pounds or 225 pounds. He wanted her body and he desired to caress her mind. He wanted to be everything to her, her priest, her provider and her protector. He wanted to love her to her depths.

He placed her legs to rest upon his shoulders and submerged his head between them. He kissed her and probed her with his tongue, tasting her from top to bottom and from left to right. She tried to back away from him and the intense pleasure his tongue was delivering to her but he was expecting that and he pulled her back towards him. There was no way she was getting away from him down on the floor.

"Oshen no, I can't, I have a..." she moaned.

"Anjelica, baby, let it happen" he said. "Hasn't it been long enough that your true needs have been unaddressed, that you've gone without true satisfaction? I just want to show you how a real man treats a woman and how somebody should have been treating you all along. Is that all right?"

He lowered his head and returned to lapping and sucking her clit like a thirsty dog. She groaned a deep groan in response when he tickled her and teased her and repeatedly wrote his first and last name on her with his tongue, claiming her as his own.

She'd been with Chance just last week but he had never made her feel like this. Oshen grabbed her tightly and rolled onto his back placing her in a sitting position on his face then inserted one finger into her ass and roused her.

She didn't like that feeling and was uncomfortable with anything inside of a place designed to push things out. She had always been curious about anal sex and how it would feel but knew instantly that would be an act she would never engage in. If his finger hurt, she could only imagine how painful a dick would feel

Gigi sighed and reached behind her to grab his dick but he grabbed her hands and held them to her thighs, refusing to allow her to touch him. He had taken the hint and removed his finger from her ass but also prevented all ways of escape and all methods of distraction leaving her to concentrate on the vast oral pleasure he was delivering to her body.

She twisted and turned and jerked against his face before finally exploding and screaming out into the atmosphere of the lavish guest room with wave after wave of carnality. Her body trembled and shook uncontrollably and he drank the sweetest nectar he'd ever tasted in his life.

She sat there on his chest and let the glow of ecstasy continue to wash over her while he traced the inside of her thighs with his finger. He had awakened senses on her body she never knew she had and she found herself suspended in a true state of euphoria.

When she finally tried to stand on rickety legs that felt like spaghetti he refused to let her up and pulled her back down onto his face. She had climaxed all over him but he wasn't done and he resumed his erotic assault on her body, pressing his tongue flat against her still swollen, hyper-sensitive clit.

His magical tongue sought to give her a second release and she finally rewarded his efforts handsomely. The second explosion finally erupted, this one more powerful than the first and he licked up every drop then she rolled off of him and collapsed.

He laid her back on her back and knelt over her to kiss every exposed inch of her body until he once again reached her mouth and those luscious, thick lips. He kissed her mouth, sucked her fingers and kissed her lips again before standing up and helped her up by her hand with him.

"C'mon Girl," he said, "let's take a shower. You got me smelling like pussy."

Meanwhile, at the Office

Sydney cringed when she saw trifling Dionne approaching. She was not her favorite person by far and the two didn't get along at all. In fact, one seemed to always go out of their way to insult the other.

"Hey Sydney girl" purred Dionne, "ain't it a awesome morning?" she continued

"Isn't it an" replied Sydney.

"Excuse me" asked Dionne with much attitude.

She was certain this basic broad who obviously didn't know how to please her man wasn't trying to correct her speech.

"An awesome morning" said Sydney. "You said ain't it a awesome morning. Isn't, dear. Isn't it *an* awesome morning" corrected Sydney.

"Whatever, heffa" Dionne sucked her teeth and strutted away.

The *last* thing Sydney needed to do was check her on anything. She hoped Sydney liked how her pussy tasted on Tim's lips last night or this morning or whenever his ass got home if he went home at all.

She laughed silently to herself and smiled. The way Dionne spoke was the very least of that dumb broad's problems. She could think of at least one thing she *should* be focused on.

Sydney hated Dionne. The woman reeked of side-piece, her speech said side-piece, her walk said side-piece, she was a home-wrecking side-piece and it irked Sydney beyond measure.

It was this kind of so-called woman that forced Sydney to agree to an open marriage. She knew Tim had a roving eye and would eventually do more than just look. So she very reluctantly entered into an agreement with him that drastically changed the dynamic of their relationship.

He was allowed to enjoy the company of any woman he chose with the only stipulation being he had to always make sure Sydney came first, her needs were always met and he would never catch feelings.

She hated it. She couldn't sleep at night when he was out. The only positive she could find was she knew where he was most of the time but lately, he'd taken to sneaking off and disappearing and she *didn't* know where he was. That bothered her and she was certain there was a woman involved but it wasn't anyone they'd talked about or agreed upon.

After seventeen years of marriage and their agreement there was no reason he should be sneaking around having secret affairs, no reason at all. The irony was she wasn't allowed to entertain side men. Any man she dealt with he would have wanted to turn into a threesome. He would have wanted to choose him, be there, and stipulate only he could enter her.

She didn't understand why there were so many restrictions applied to her but he could basically do whatever he pleased. He had many affairs throughout the years but she had none.

She glanced up at the clock and wondered where Gigi was. Gigi wasn't the kind to be late, not even in inclement weather.

The last time Sydney spoke with her, she had escaped the clutches of Evan Beauchamp and somehow wound up in the company of Oshen Benjamin. Those were two crazy fine individuals. She didn't comprehend why Gigi always seemed to attract the handsomest men in existence but they were never worth a wooden nickel nor two dead flies.

She remembered she told her about a guy she met in middle school named Scott. A few years after high school graduation, they dated and in doing so, she found herself in the middle of a demoralizing and embarrassing crazy threesome. She always regretted not having the guts to say "No" and now more than twenty-five years later, Scott still told different variations of that old story to *whomever* would listen. That was probably his greatest sexual achievement in an otherwise lackluster and dismal life. Why would he continue to talk about it otherwise?

And of course there was the in-secure, adulterous, arrogant, pompous, womanizing, manipulative, abusive minister she messed around and married. Gigi first met him at the same middle school where she met Scott. She couldn't think of enough negative adjectives to describe that jerk preacher or minister or whatever he called himself these days. She wondered if people were ordaining and licensing themselves. She couldn't imagine any pastor worth his salt would title *that* guy.

He was the biggest loser of all, a total waste of time and space and to top it off, he wasn't even fine! Syd was ecstatic when Gigi divorced him after discovering an affair that had to be at least 3 years at the time. The abuse killed that marriage and the affair put the nail in the coffin. The other woman Gigi caught him with was married and divorced her husband to be with the fake. She and Gigi laughed to the point of crying many days wondering how long it took Kim to realize the huge mistake she had made divorcing her husband for the loser/monster/adulterer. She got what she asked for they rationalized and so did he.

Sydney hoped and prayed her best friend never ran into another man from that school. Her track record was horrible.

She called Gigi's phone and the call went straight to voicemail. She had been with Oshen Benjamin the last time she spoke with her so she thought maybe he might know where she was. When she looked up his phone number and called him she got no answer as well.

A frustrated Sydney hung up the phone in a flurry of expletives and sent out a bunch of texts. What is the point of a cell phone if people are not going to answer them" she asked herself? People were silly.

She needed coffee and some Kahlua because everyone knows Kahlua fixed *everything*, more Kahlua than coffee though. If you were snowed in at home with a bunch of kids or a whiny husband, hot coffee and Kahlua was just the thing you needed. Frozen coffee plus Kahlua in the summertime hooked you up while you chilled on the patio. Kahlua made it all better.

"Good luck finding some Kahlua" she thought to herself and grabbed her coffee cup.

Her brain was a ball of confusion as she walked aimlessly back down the hall towards her desk after getting her coffee. Gee was missing and to top it off, Tim didn't come home last night. Perhaps that's why she didn't see Evan and Al Bernard coming her way. She collided headfirst into AB, spilling coffee all over his lambs-wool overcoat sending him into an obscenity laced tirade.

"You freaking idiot" he screamed, "watch where the fuck you're going! Is there a bird sized brain anywhere in that water ass head of yours?" She waited calmly and patiently as he continued.

"You've ruined my damn coat. You know you're paying for this shit, right?"

Sydney stood silently. She was like water in a tea kettle sitting on the stove. Any minute now that kettle was going to whistle.

"Hello" he said and snapped his fingers in her face.

"Are you done" she asked with an eerie placidity.

"Done" he screamed, "Done? I won't be done until I have your job, you rude, incompetent wench?! Don't just stand there looking stupid!! Say something!"

"Oh, so I have your permission to speak now" she asked.

He had no idea exactly who he was dealing with or what he was setting himself up for. He opened the floodgates and unleashed Typhoon Sydney and once that thing escaped its confines, it would be almost impossible to put it back in.

"I don't know who the fuck you think you're talking to like that but I'm not the motherfucking one! You're standing there acting like that piece of shit coat costs thousands!! Punk its fucking lambs-wool, it cost you $200, maybe $300 tops" she said. "Where the hell do you get off, telling me what the hell I'm gonna do? Now what I *will* do, is go and get you fifty dollars to clean the motherfucker but I'm not replacing shit! Have a good got damn day."

He stood with his mouth gawked open as she side-stepped him and angrily walked away. No one had ever spoken to him like that before, no one ever stood up to him. He found her erotic and he found himself turned on in every way. He wanted to take her right then and there, dick her down and make her call him Daddy.

"Damn" Evan exclaimed "she checked your ass!!" He threw his head back and laughed aloud.

"How many times do I have to tell you about trying to check these females out here, Man" he chided and continued on to their appointment.

The receptionist escorted them to Charla's office and Evan teased and admonished him the whole way. He'd encountered Sydney and her mouth before but AB started in on her so quickly, he didn't have the time to warn him about her.

"Mr. Beauchamp, Mr. Bernard" greeted Charla, "welcome and allow me to apologize for Mrs. Taylor's behavior. You are most definitely assured that this *is* her final day with Glass Slipper Media."

"It's all good Charla, that won't be necessary" Evan said. "If anyone should be apologizing it should be old AB here. He's the one who started it" said Evan with a chuckle. "It's all good now let's get these papers signed. I'm ready to go on the road!"

Normally, the Artist and the promoter would never meet face-to-face. That's what Managers and Agents were for. Evan must have had an ulterior motive for coming into her office.

He did. He wanted to see Gigi again. They went over the contract terms and Evan surprisingly requested that Charla send Gigi to Las Vegas on opening night as a rider. That wasn't Gigi's department and she didn't perform in that capacity, she tried in vain to explain but she had to serve up Gigi or no deal.

It was a very strange request, one that caused her to wonder if that had anything to do with Gigi calling in sick today, especially since she and Evan had that meeting last night. Her thoughts were interrupted by Sydney's knock at the door.

"Mr. Bernard, here's fifty-dollars to clean your overcoat, just as I promised. Please reach out if that isn't enough to cover your expenses." She was being extra nice and courteous. They were in her boss's boss's office, after all.

"Ms...I'm sorry I didn't get your name" he said.

"Mrs. Mrs. Zanchak-Taylor" snapped Sydney.

She wasn't going to allow him to disrespect her or her marriage. He should have been very glad they were in Charla's office or she would have given him her entire backside to kiss. He was a pompous jerk and she was *not* feeling him at all.

"Mrs. Zanchak, would you do me the honor of having lunch with me? I was a little rough earlier and I'd like to make it up to you."

"That would be Zanchak-Taylor and I've told you that before. I never entertain men alone without my husband, so thank you but no" Sydney said. This guy was ridiculous. He made her butthole itch with his silly self.

"You're an absolutely gorgeous woman, Mrs. Zanchak. You look just like my second wife."

"Damn, how many times have you been married" inquired Sydney.

"Once" he answered.

Sydney sucked her teeth and left the office in a huff.

AB was fascinated with Sydney. He liked the challenge that she presented and he was going to have a good time breaking her down and taming her.

She didn't know it yet but whether she had a husband or not, he was going to have her and he plotted his plan in his head. He got her first name from the front desk receptionist and put his plan into action before he left the office.

Later that afternoon

It was 1:00 in the afternoon and Sydney perused a few delivery menus from some local eateries to order lunch. She was tired of the same mundane food options available to her in downtown Cleveland. She grabbed her bag and headed for the little deli in the lobby for a good ole Cleveland corned beef sandwich. She would eat lunch in Gigi's office by herself.

"I was just on my way to get you" said Erica.

She was one of the receptionists from the front desk. She was young and fresh and Sydney liked her a lot.

"You got roses, Girl! A whole bunch of 'em! Here's the card" she exclaimed.

Two delivery men made four trips to deliver eight different floral arrangements of orange roses. Sydney smiled to herself. She had the best husband in the world. She knew all along that he'd apologize for not coming home last night but this was way over the top. It made her wonder what he actually did that made him go to these lengths to apologize.

All of the women in the office crowded around her to admire the wonderful expression of love Tim had bestowed upon her. She opened the card and began to read aloud.

"My sincerest apologies to the most beautiful woman I've ever laid eyes on. Alfred Bernard" the card read.

Sydney let out an audible gasp and clasped her hand over her mouth as she stood in total shock. She couldn't accept a gift this extravagant from a man that wasn't her husband.

"Yawl get this bullshit off my damn desk! Take whatever the hell you want just make sure it's all gone by the time I get back from lunch" she screamed.

"Um, Sydney" Erica began, "Micah Asher's is here with lunch from Mr. Bernard."

"You eat it" she snapped back.

"I can't, he's it's for the whole office. It's in the 9th Street conference room."

Sydney rushed over to the conference room where there were trays of Lobster Mac and Cheese, Roasted Broccoli and Prime Rib carved by a chef. There was a table filled with Cannoli, various cheesecakes and Molten Lava cake and a wait staff in place to serve and clean up afterwards. One of the waiters handed Sydney another card from Al Bernard but this one she did not read aloud.

"I'll do this kind of thing every day until you agree to have dinner with me privately, Pretty Lady. Signed AB."

She was stunned. No one, not even her husband had gone this far to impress her. She wasn't sure who this Al Bernard person really was but if he'd gone through that much trouble to get her attention, he may be worthy of a second look, whether she had a husband or not.

Dionne, of course, wasted no time sneaking off to a quiet corner to text Tim.

"Your whore is cheating on your ass" she texted, "because I know your stingy ass didn't buy this whole office lunch from Micah Asher's" she continued, "and eight dozen orange roses, too?"

"Who? Somebody sent roses to *my* wife?" questioned Tim.

"You saw exactly what the fuck I just said" she answered. "Looks like somebody been hitting that to me. You'd better step your game up playboy, that's all I'm saying."

"I ain't got to step up shit, my shit is tight" he texted back. "I'm on my damn way down there anyway, damn it."

"If you say so…"

"I do say so…what you doing tonight?"

"You" she answered him.

"You know the drill. Ass-naked, eight o'clock." he texted and turned off his phone.

Dionne created drama purposely. Sydney shouldn't be so stank all the time. She quietly smiled to herself on her way back to her desk. Payback is a mean, funky bitch.

WHEN A MAN WANTS A WOMAN

Right around 3:00 p.m.

Tim Taylor was enraged! He was on his way to Sydney's job and she had better have answers when he got there. Whoever this man was sending his wife flowers had either already had her or was trying his damnedest to get her. He wanted answers and he wanted them now.

Sydney knew the rules of engagement. If he wasn't there to watch, she could not entertain another man. If he didn't choose him for her, she could not entertain another man. Nothing happened without his approval but some random dude was showering her with flowers and buying lunch for her friends. *That* was a man with a motive and *that* had to be stopped. She had better have some answers.

"What's up Erica" greeted Tim, "Sydney around? Tell her I'm here to take her to lunch."

"She's in a meeting with Charla and a Client, Mr. Taylor" replied Erica "and I expect it'll last through the end of the work day." she told him. "Unfortunately, I can't disturb her. I'll tell her you were here though."

Erica covered for people in the office hundreds of times before. She didn't think Sydney had done anything wrong but the look in Tim's eyes frightened her so she trusted her intuition and turned him away.

He left the office seething. There should be no client, meeting, or anything else that should take precedence over him. Some dude is sending her flowers, buying her lunch and now she's too busy with her silly meeting for her husband?

He knew what the problem was: she spent too much time with that Anjelica Haralson and on this trivial job. He asked her several times to quit and help him run *his* business but his silly ass wife was busy helping someone else run theirs.

If Tim weren't 100 percent sure Sydney had never been with a woman, he would swear she was strapping up and screwing Gigi. They spent more time together than he and his wife did and Tim was tired of it.

That lonely broad didn't have a man, couldn't keep a man and when she did have one he wasn't worth half a damn. His wife was getting beside herself and Tim had to reign her but in the meantime…

"Excuse me, Ms. It isn't my intention to disturb you but your smile lit up the entire lobby. It is stunningly beautiful. May I ask you your name" asked Tim as he approached the most beautiful woman he'd ever seen. Today anyway.

Chapter 5

Clean as A Whistle

That same afternoon

Oshen and Gigi sat in the driveway at her condo. Her truck was still in its place, undisturbed but the box of roses was gone from the street.

The HOA association had undoubtedly cleaned it up and she knew the ridiculous bill would come soon. She hated her HOA and its strict rules. Soon, they'll be telling her she had to get married and have a baby or be fined.

She looked at Oshen out of the corner of her eye and instantly decided to friend zone him. He had never been married, had no kids and had a squeaky clean public image. The media couldn't even find a traffic ticket against him. He was a strikingly handsome man but at 13 years her junior, far too young for her to seriously entertain.

"C'mon Babe, there's the police" he said as a police cruiser appeared in the rearview mirror. He helped her out of the truck and they both walked over and greeted Officer Addison.

She was extremely grateful to Oshen for taking control of the situation and she felt more comfortable with him than she did with any man before. He had her best interests at heart. That was new to her and she didn't know exactly what to do with those kinds of feelings.

In the past, she'd always been on her own, even when she was married. *That* selfish bastard protected only his own interests. She couldn't explain how she was so sure so early but Oshen had her back.

Gigi opened the front door of the condo and little Vongi raced out. The purebred Yorkie missed his mommy and tried to climb up her leg. She bent down to pick up the little dog when Oshen snatched her out of the doorway and shielded her with his body. He hadn't remembered hearing the dog bark last night nor did he remember it meeting them at the door.

Officer Addison drew his weapon and entered first. He identified himself, ensured the house was secure and then allowed them inside.

They were stunned. This was not the scene they left behind last night. The foyer was immaculate and there wasn't a smudge on the mirror or a mark on the floor. Everything was in its place. Someone cleaned the nightmarish sight just as they had set it up in the first place.

He turned to Gigi and saw her fraying at the edges and although he was shaken too, he was the only thing preventing *her* from falling apart. He had to maintain his composure for her.

They thanked Officer Addison for coming out and went back in to wait for Brenda Welch, the realtor. There was no report to file so there was no need to hold the officer. All evidence of any foul play had long been removed.

"Baby? You okay" Oshen asked.

"Yes" she replied, "I'm fine."

She wasn't fine, she was irritated. He wasn't her man and she didn't like him calling her baby. She also didn't like the fact that he was pushing her to sell her condo and she really didn't want to sell. It was hers, there was no mortgage and she didn't *want* to move. She also didn't like him taking control of her life, restricting her movements or dressing her like a 2-year-old. He was over-stepping his boundaries and it was time for him to exit her life, stage left.

"Oshen, I got it from here" she told him, "you can take off. We'll talk tomorrow. Do me a favor and lock the door on your way out."

"Girl you're crazy" he replied, "Ain't no way I'm leaving you here all by yourself."

"Oshen, get the fuck out" she screamed, "*Now!*"

She ran up the stairs to her bedroom, two at a time with Oshen close behind. Her body quivered as she collapsed into his arms, weeping uncontrollably.

"It's okay, Baby girl, it's okay. I got you" he said to her and kissed the top of her head, "I got you."

Thursday November 6, 2014

Two nights after her encounter with that ridiculous Evan, Gigi headed to church. The past 40 hours had her a complete mess and she sought refuge, a place where she could find solace, where she could hear herself think. The message from the pulpit, the love from the people, the music, it all made her feel better.

Gigi knew that God loved her. Sure she disappointed Him regularly but He continued to love her nonetheless and she continued to serve and worship whenever time allowed. Hopefully her schedule would open up and that would change soon.

"I know, I know Grams" she thought to herself, "God should always be first in all things. No excuses."

She couldn't wait for her schedule to open up and then try to fit God into it. That was backwards and her Grams had taught her better. She had to schedule her schedule around God not the other way around.

She sat as far back in the comfortable rows of seats as she could so as not to attract the attention of the Prophet. She came to this place of worship only for the music she rationalized. She was going through it and could really use the prayer but the leaders at *this* church always told your business first and she wanted none of that she told herself. She was glad they weren't like that at *her* church.

The truth of the matter was before she'd gotten all high and mighty and important, she'd been a worship leader.

She sat in the back because she was hiding and she didn't want to be called out for it. She sighed to herself. She really was running.

As the Prophet began to teach, she slid the usher an offering envelope and slipped out the door. It was getting late and she had to go to work in the morning.

She smiled to herself as she remembered how the old folks used to pronounce the word "usher" incorrectly and say "ur-sher". She had fond memories of growing up Holiness with all of its traditions and rules and regulations. They were comical to her now but she appreciated them because that was what helped to shape her and she had a solid life foundation because of it. Her grandmother used to always say holiness is right. Never had a truer statement been uttered than that.

Once outside, she plugged up her cell and turned it on. Oshen had called her about ten times and Sydney had too. There was a call from her idiot ex-husband's punk behind and Evan as well. She didn't want to talk to anyone, she simply wanted to go somewhere by herself, sit and gather her thoughts.

She let the car warm up a bit and sat and argued with herself.

"How the hell did *that* idiot get my *personal* cell?"

"You gave it to him, you must have."

"No, I didn't. I was trying to get away from that fool, and I wasn't trying to make conversation and exchange telephone numbers."

"Maybe he Facebooked you. That messenger app lists your phone number doesn't it? How else can people call you if it doesn't?"

"That may be it. Wait, no. I don't have that app for that very reason. People know I have working relationships with celebrities and I don't want Flirt and Debel-Dit and Lovaty and Tootie and 'nem from back in the day hitting me up on some thirsty shit. Damn it, now I have to change my number. I hate that man"

She drove the long way back to the house and wondered in the back of her mind exactly what methods Evan's hungry, pressed behind used to get her personal phone number. That's why she didn't initially notice the lights behind her shadowing her every move. She'd already traveled a few miles when she originally saw them.

At first, she dismissed it as the local paparazzi trying to get the scoop on who was gallivanting around town in Killer Wave's car. Oshen had vanity plates on the BMW Roadster she was driving and it was common knowledge in Northeast Ohio who the car with Numba33 plates belonged to. She hadn't thought of that before but it was far too late now.

She turned left and the lights behind her turned left as well. She continued about a mile and turned right, watching in the rearview mirror as the lights behind her followed suit. There was no doubt about it: she was being followed.

She peeled a sharp left into oncoming traffic, with tires screeching on the wet asphalt and floored the gas pedal through a middle class neighborhood. She gripped the steering wheel so tightly blood flow to her fingers was restricted and they had become numb.

She sped through the quiet, tree-lined streets of modest homes, fish-tailing on the poorly plowed side streets. She tried her best not to hit stray cars parked on the streets and surprisingly maintained control of the little sports car. She skidded into a hairpin U-turn on a boulevard then straightened the car to get back to the clear and safer main thoroughfare.

She turned around to look behind her and dread seized her heart. The car was still close behind and gaining ground. She blew through the red light at the intersection doing seventy miles per hour but the suspect car relentlessly gave pursuit. She was petrified but in her strength answered the hands free telephone system in the car.

"Oh, so we're ignoring phone calls now" Oshen asked uncomfortably.

"Someone's following me" she wailed. Her hands were shaking, she was hyperventilating and he could hear the panic in her voice. He tried to draw her focus to him and away from the danger behind her.

"Okay Baby girl, listen to me. Pull into the parking lot at the next gas station you see. Okay? Will you do that for me" he asked in the most relaxing soothing voice he could muster.

Gas station parking lots were always well lit no matter the time of day or night and they also had surveillance cameras. There was a slim chance of catching the guy on tape but a 100% chance that she would be safe and off the roads until he could get to her.

"I don't see one" she cried as she sped through the red light at the intersection. Red and blues lights appeared in her rearview mirror and forced her to pull to the side of the road. She heard the other car screech to a halt to prevent breaching the intersection and the whole terrifying ordeal came to an abrupt end.

"Anjelica, what's going on? Where are you" asked a worried Oshen.

"The police just pulled me over, I'll be all right. I'm at Mayfield and Richmond in Lyndhurst I think or maybe Mayfield Heights. There's a BP on the other side of the light and I think that's City Hall or the Board of Education or some shit across from the BP. Hell, I'm so confused, I don't know but I'll be there shortly" she said.

Gigi was a nervous wreck on the side of the road in the little Z4 Roadster. She gathered herself and gave him her exact location and felt much better knowing he was in route. She thanked God for the police lights flashing behind her as they may have saved her life.

It seemed as if every car in town was slowing down and snapping cell phone pictures as they passed by Numba33's car. Chance was no exception as he too rubbernecked and honked his horn as he rode by in his Chrysler 300.

Gigi was furious. Was *he* the idiot bastard who had been following her? He probably enjoyed every lunatic minute of the twisted game he just engaged her in. She couldn't believe he took time out of his day to harass her like that. At least it wasn't a crazy stalker chasing her through Cleveland Heights. She could at least take comfort in that fact.

Chapter 6

Making His Move

Sunday November 9, 2014

It was Sunday morning and for Oshen that meant Game day. He stayed at the team hotel the night before as was customary. The practice eliminated late arrivals, players being stopped by police or accidents happening on game days. They were not a playoff caliber team and if they were going to post a respectable record this season, they couldn't lose personnel to simple things like police stops. The Cleveland Lightening needed all hands on deck.

Sleep had escaped him. He tossed and turned all night with visions of her naked body reacting to his tongue dancing through his head and the memory of the way her fat, pendulous breasts spilled through his fingers and made his manhood ache and throb.

He constantly wondered if she was okay knowing the events of the past few days had left them both a bit shaken. The black roses and snakes did it for him, being chased through the city streets did it for her.

He gave her the keys to his more understated and common Mercedes C350. He felt much better with her driving that car than any of the others as it didn't have vanity plates and wouldn't draw any more unwanted and unnecessary attention.

He reached for the phone to call her after which he'd hit the shower. He wanted to not only hear her voice but also confirm she had all of the information she'd need to access the Players' Guest areas like access passes, parking passes, ID, the normal stuff.

He wanted to hear her voice too. Her phone went to voicemail as usual and he listened to the whole message as usual. Her voice exuded power, confidence, polish and determination. His dick stiffened and he reached into his fitted boxer briefs and grabbed it under the cover.

"Hey Bro?! Get the fuck out of here with the bullshit, Man" his roommate yelled for the bathroom, "do that shit in the shower, nasty motherfucker".

He'd forgotten he wasn't alone and lost himself in the complete essence of her and the euphoria he felt a few days ago of being with her.

"Don't get yourself in no bullshit today, Baby girl" he thought to himself.

He couldn't put on his "S" shirt for her for a few hours. He had to focus on what he was being paid so many millions of dollars to do. Oshen Benjamin was a straight savage on a football field and no woman, not even her, was going to distract him and change that, ever.

It was time to transform from Oshen Benjamin to the awed, the feared Killer Wave. He'd catch up with her after the game.

Sunday about 11:00 a.m.

Gigi lazily sauntered into the quaint Tremont cafe on the near west side of Cleveland within a short distance of the football stadium. This little meeting needed to be quick. She didn't want to be late for her first ever professional football game and besides, Sydney and Tim couldn't get in without her. She knew she was a little lulu to have agreed to breakfast with this cretin yet here she was walking towards the table where the jerk sat. Evan stood to greet her.

"Thank you for joining me, Beautiful" he said and pulled out her chair, "I appreciate it."

"Not a problem" she answered, "but call me Gigi. How can I help you today?"

"Well, Anjelica you can help me by forgiving me for my inappropriate behavior a few nights ago. It was out of line, out of character and I'm sorry."

"No need to apologize, all's forgiven. Now if you'll excuse me" she said and stood up to leave.

"What's your rush" he asked, "you haven't had breakfast yet" he said and tugged at her arm. "Please do me this one honor?"

"Okay Oshen...I mean Evan, but keep your mouth and your hands to yourself" she warned. "I don't want to have to smack the shit out of you in front of all these lovely people this morning" she said and smiled sarcastically.

She called him Oshen and it made him cringe. He laughed out loud to mask his disgust with her mistake although he wasn't sure that it *was* a mistake and he was correct with that realization. She was well aware of the source of the conflict between the two of them and she threw a low blow when she called him Oshen.

"So Gigi, tell me something about you I don't know. Give me the dirt on who Anjelica Haralson really is" he said.

"Not much to tell" she expressed and ordered: Two sausage patties, hash brown potatoes with onions, cheese and green peppers, an asiago cheese bagel, a glass of coffee with half hot chocolate, cream and ice and a bowl of fresh fruit.

"I'm the third of four children, the second of three girls. I grew up without my father, money was tight but my momma dug in deep and did what she had to do. End of story" she said and sipped her coffee drink. It needed more ice and she waved over the waiter.

"Tell me this" Evan uttered.

"No, my turn" replied Gigi slyly. "What happened to end your last relationship" she questioned and anxiously anticipated his response.

She liked asking men that question because it gave her tons of insight into who she was dealing with.

"To be honest" Evan began, "we grew apart and before I knew it, she was in someone else's bed and so was

I." He ran his hand down his mouth and goatee, sat back in his
chair, then let out a long sigh.

"She caught us and beat us both down, never mind the fact that she was smashing another nig…I mean another man. Anyway, I pushed her to get her off of me and the next thing I knew, I was cuffed in the back of a police car on my way to lockup."

Gigi had no intention whatsoever of seeing this man ever again in any capacity. He had a propensity for violence and she wanted none of it.

There was a very uneasy silence hovering over the two of them. She was done with the conversation and *refused* to waste another moment of her precious time. She had tons of other things she needed to do, none of which included this idiot.

On the outside, Evan Beauchamp was everything a woman wanted in a man but his inside left much to be desired. With those few words, he'd revealed himself to be dishonest, a liar, a cheater, hot-tempered, abusive and a man who doesn't take responsibility for his own actions.

"Well Evan, thank you so much for breakfast" she said and reached for her bag. She took out her wallet and left money on the table for her portion of the meal.

Evan maintained his composure but his displeasure was obvious. One thing he did not need was this woman's money. He wasn't a scrub so how dare she treat him like one. This date wasn't over until he said it was over and whether she knew it or not, this *was* a date. She wasn't going anywhere and she damn sure wasn't going to throw her money in his face like he was some basic bum dude.

"Wait a minute Beautiful, I planned something really nice for after breakfast. Where are you going so fast" he asked and grabbed her wrist.

She looked down at his hand. Her first instinct was to punch him square dead in his face but there was a great probability that he would hit her back. She kept her hands to herself and grinned at Evan broadly. She then leaned over to whisper in his ear so that only he could hear her:

"Let go of my fucking arm or I will make a scene and *your* pretty ass will be fodder for every tabloid, gossip blog, TMZ and social networking site known to man" she whispered through clenched teeth.

He locked his eyes with hers and tightened his grip.

"Let me *GO!*" she yelled and jerked away.

Her outburst attracted the attention of the patrons in the Café but she didn't care. She warned him before about putting his hands on her before and there he went and did it again. She snatched her bag, rolled her eyes and stormed out of the door.

"May I have the check please" he asked his waiter. "That went well" he said to himself as he sipped his coffee. Back to the drawing board.

Game time: 1:00 p.m.

Gigi, Sydney and Tim settled into their seats in the luxury suite Oshen shared with two other Lightening team mate. The suite held about 30 people which included, the other players' wife and girlfriend as well as various family members and friends

"Girl? This is nice. Who knew rich people had it this good" declared Sydney as she wiggled in her very comfortable cushioned seat. She was as giddy as a kid on opening presents on Christmas morning taking in the luxury of it all.

She looked around and admired the pecan cabinets and the plush leather seating. The recessed lighting cast a warming glow on the butter pecan colored walls which complimented the pecan cabinetry and woodwork throughout the suite.

There was free food but not your typical stadium food. There was an omelet station with selections that included crab, chorizo, spinach, grilled portabellas, tomatoes, Pico de Gallo, caramelized onions, asparagus, cheddar and feta cheeses to name a few.

There was a pasta station with cavatelli, cheese tortellini, pesto, marinara sauce, roasted garlic cream sauce, grilled chicken, Italian sausage, sautéed vegetables, Italian bread, hot pepper dipping oil and freshly grated parmesan cheese and seafood offerings of middle neck clams and grilled shrimp with redskin potatoes, cream corn, smoked kielbasa, and white bean, bacon and kale soup.

The beverage options included Corona Extra®, Patron Silver®, Grand Marnier® and pitchers of Margaritas.

The rank and file paid an arm and a leg for hot dogs and soda while the rich didn't shell out a dime for Chilled and Grilled shrimp and blue crab hushpuppies amongst other gourmet fare. No wonder rich people stayed rich; they didn't have to pay for anything.

"Tim, Baby you straight, do you need anything" Sydney attended to her husband. He was already nursing a beer and exchanging glances with a blue-eyed brunette across the room, which made her stomach churn.

"As a matter of fact, I do; I need a bite of that right there" he whispered and nodded his head in the direction of the smiling brunette.

"Babe not today okay, just not today. We came here to have a good time" Sydney stressed.

She was tired of knowingly sharing her husband and she figured the woman to be a call girl anyway. She'd never liked it but he was going to do him whether she liked it or not.

At the outset of the open marriage concept, she thought she would be okay with knowing where he was and who he was with but it didn't turn out that way. Knowing had become the source of many sleepless nights and at times, like now, the thought made her flat out sick.

"My wife can't possibly be telling me no, because my wife knows I'm a grown ass man and I'll do what the fuck I want to. As a matter of fact, bring your ass because I'm sick of playing with you and your bullshit ass stuck-up ass attitude. If *you* don't give me my threesome another bitch will and you'd better believe that" he snarled.

He got up and left the room and soon after the brunette followed suit. Perhaps she was trying to be discreet but both she and Gigi knew what was about to go down.

"Sydney, what *exactly* was *that* all about" asked Gigi and leaned in close.

"*That* is the biggest mistake I've *ever* made as it pertains to this marriage" she said and shifted in her chair to face Gigi.

"I love Timlin Taylor" Sydney said and twirled her hair around her finger "and I don't want to lose him but I'm nearing the end of my rope. He came to me about fifteen years ago asking for permission to spend the night with another woman. *He* said it would be a good thing for our marriage. He said it wasn't cheating if I knew where he was or who he was with and I agreed to that bullshit and ever since, he's been fucking other bitches right in my face. He tries to give me a spoonful of sugar with the nasty ass medicine by saying there is nothing stopping me from doing it too but I call bullshit. I know this motherfucker been fucking some damn body without my damn permission and I'm sick of the bullshit for real. He keeps trying to drag me into a trifling ass threesome, you saw how he just told me to come on. He wanted me to fuck that broad with him. Time out for this dumb ass shit, I ain't on it."

Gigi was stunned. Sydney was strong, outspoken and seemed to be very secure within herself. Their marriage looked perfect from the outside looking in and she had a hard time processing her actually sharing a man.

"Shocking huh? Me and my say-something-and-I'll-fuck-you-up, strong self, sharing a man don't even sound right, does it? You ain't telling me *shit* I don't already know" Sydney said after reading Gigi's mind, "but you know what, I just might take Al Bernard up on his offer."

"What's Al Bernard got to do with anything and what offer are you talking about" inquired a confused Gigi.

"Girl? I didn't tell you about that" asked Sydney.

"Um, No! You most certainly did *not*" replied Gigi.

"Well damn, that's what the fuck happens when your silly ass don't answer the got damn phone. Anyway, that fool tried to check me Friday and I had to get right with his ass.

Long story short, he sent me like eight dozen roses and bought lunch for the whole office girl, from Asher Micah's of all places, talking about he'll keep sending roses and buying lunch until I go out with him" Sydney explained.

"You're playing with me, right? Sydney, that dude is married I think. As a matter of fact, I'm sure of it" said Gigi.

"Ain't nobody trying to marry the man but if Tim's ass can play why I can't? I have never stepped out on him with or without permission but I'm really sick of watching him and his parade of whores from the sidelines. I think it's about time he tags me in."

"Oh my god, that is way too much drama for me for one day. I actually have a little tea of my own this afternoon" said Gigi. "You know Evan asked me to meet him for breakfast this morning to apologize for acting a damn fool the other night but the idiot had the unmitigated gall to grab me when I stood up to leave. Girl that fool just didn't know how much danger he was really in, putting his damn hands on me."

"See shit like that is why you should let me go ahead and introduce you to Orlando. He's a good dude, trust me on this" Sydney whispered.

Gigi snapped her head to look Sydney in the eye.

"Syd no and that's final! Let's drop this topic of conversation because I am really sick of visiting it with you. Is he black? Is he rocking that caramel mocha skin I adore so much? If not that subject is closed, been closed and needs to stay closed. You're on my first and last nerve with that" she exclaimed.

"Okay, all right, it's closed for right now anyway" Sydney said.

She shook her head at her friend. That girl was crazy.

"So while you're so concerned with hooking me up, what *exactly* did you mean you might take Al Bernard up on his offer? Take him up how, married lady?"

"What do you think" Syd said with a raised eyebrow.

"I don't know heffa, that's why I'm asking."

"If you have to ask Ms. Saved-Sanctified-and Filled with the Holy Ghost, your ass don't need to know" Syd said and shook her head.

The two of them settled in and began to have a really good time, once the game got going but Tim was still noticeably absent.

Oshen was having a classic Killer Wave game. He had 15 carries for 72 yards and that was before the half. He was the obvious love child of Tony Dorsett and Earl Campbell, if there could be such a thing and Gigi was proud. She and Sydney were screaming his name louder than anyone else in the stands or the suite.

"Excuse me, Ma'am? My name is Bambi. Bambi Dough. Are you Oshen's mother" the young woman asked Gigi.

She looked to be in her mid-twenties and was the Real Housewives of Wherever surgically beautiful. The way Gigi and Sydney were cheering for Oshen, the young woman was convinced they were family members.

"I'm a really, really good friend of Oshen's and it's so good to finally meet you" she said and extended her hand to Gigi.

This girl clearly had it wrong but Gigi went ahead and played along anyway.

"You're not serious are you? Your name isn't really Bambi Dough, is it" she asked the young woman who continued to stand there thunderstruck and totally confused.

Why did people insist on naming their children those stupid, idiotic names? What kind of a job could a grown woman ever get with a silly name like that? There would be Stripper, Porn Star or Call Girl and that would about run the gamut.

"Never mind" Gigi said with a flick of the hand. She decided to have a little fun.

"Ms. Dough, Oshen has never made mention of you to me before. Exactly how long have you supposedly been dating?"

"Gigi" Sydney cried, "tell this little girl to get on some damn where."

She looked at Sydney and giggled. The woman was crazy. She was sure of it.

"Look Honey" Sydney said, "*this* ain't his Momma. As a matter of fact, he's trying to get her to let him stand up in it. Now take your little pencil thin self on and play with your other Barbie looking friend some damn where now. We're trying to watch the game, Baby."

"What do you mean stand up in it" Bambi asked with a perplexed look on her face.

"What kind of backwoods, rocking chair, porch sitting, country ass shit is that?"

The light bulb in her ditzy head finally clicked and she looked mortified.

You mean he's trying to screw *your* old rusty ass? You're kidding right? Oh My God, that's disgusting! There's probably cobwebs and dust all up in that ancient ass, dry ass pussy" Bambi said and high-fived on of her girlfriends over her shoulder.

The woman reminded Gigi of an old Bratz doll with her too full lips and set apart eyes. No matter what happened, Gigi would never enhance her lips. *That* woman looked crazy

"If that pussy *is* dry it would be because Oshen sucked the lining out of it, now I'm tired of playing with you, little girl. Get the hell on up out of here before I grind your ass up hurt your little feelings up in here. Now go the fuck on" Sydney warned.

"First, check yourself because you ain't never just goin' grind me up and I'm just goin' take it. Shit ain't going down like you think. I'm leaving but only because I *refuse* to act any kind of fool and embarrass Oshen *but* he *will* hear about this. You've got the game twisted, pathetic old damn women. Ain't no way and I do mean no damn way I let Granny Miller and her nursing home crew step into my domain and call themselves taking the man I worked so hard to get. You *will* see me again bitches, believe that shit" she declared and walked away.

"What I miss" Tim asked and slid in next to Sydney at the end of the encounter. She looked at him and rolled her eyes.

"The question should be what did I miss? You enjoy your little escapade" she asked.

He scowled at her with a sideways glance and she squirmed anxiously in her seat. After a few unsettling seconds, he looked away without speaking a word.

He didn't know this brand new Sydney. He didn't know this stranger that liked to challenge him all the time, this lady that liked to test his patience, this woman who told him "no" far too often. She was becoming too much like Gigi and was really starting to work his nerves. She'd better take a long hard look at that broad. There was a reason she didn't have a husband and if Sydney didn't watch it, she wouldn't have one either.

Monday November 17, 2014

Chance Williams ran across the parking deck in the frigid morning Cleveland cold. Old Man Winter had unpacked his bags and was in town for the long-haul. The arctic cold wind blew in from Canada and mixed with the warm air from Lake Erie and created the second lake effect snow storm of the winter season.

His commute had been hairy to say the least. The wind chill factor had dipped below zero after the snow event and it was difficult to start his car. It took a couple of attempts before it finally started then he sat another ten minutes warming the engine before he finally began his journey into downtown Cleveland.

The previous day's temperature was in the upper 30's and it was raining but through the night the rain turned to freezing rain and then into snow. The snow covered ice was causing drivers to slip and slide all over the highway leaving a trail of spun out vehicles that littered the main thoroughfares of I-480 & I-77.

He hoped this was not an indication of the rest of the winter. This is what one would normally get in late

December or early January not mid-November. It was too early for these kinds of conditions.

Chance was grateful for the wisdom to leave early although he still found himself a few minutes behind schedule. He was forced to run as fast as possible to make it to the elevator on time. It was imperative that he was there no later than 8:50 a.m., not a second before and not a second after if he desired to see her again.

He missed her, a lot. He missed feeling her warm body next to his and being able to turn over in the middle of the night and enter her. There was nothing better to get a day started than his favorite, first morning sex, and he especially loved it with her. She made him wear a condom every time and that made him wonder if she were seeing Oshen Benjamin far before he saw them together.

He made it to the elevator right on time but she was nowhere to be found.

"Maybe she's running a little late" he said to himself and stood in the heat to soak up the warmth until she arrived. Wait. He didn't want to look thirsty, like he was actually waiting for her. She had to think it was coincidental when the doors opened and she saw him there.

He hopped on the elevator and rode down to Level G, up to Level 7 and over again. After the third trip, he began to feel like a stalker.

"Monday" he thought to himself. He'd meet her on Monday for sure.

He peered through the dim light in the parking garage when he started to leave and saw her approaching. There was no mistaking her walk and the way she seemed to glide through the air like an angel. He pulled his hat down, stepped back into the elevator and rode to the top floor.

Gigi hoped the elevator car took its sweet time today. She wanted to revel in the heat and warm up a bit before exposing her extremities to the brutal lake effect elements all over again. There was nothing like the welcoming blast of heat after the cold has feloniously assaulted you in the dead of winter. Unless one has experienced lake effect cold, one truly cannot relate.

She had no such luck this morning as the bell rang almost immediately. She stepped inside and her eyes fell upon him and she inhaled to take in his scent. She speculated if he was taken and glanced over at his hand from the corner of her eye. She saw no ring or ring line and ascertained that he was not married but that didn't mean he was available. He might already have a girlfriend, a wife, be gay or all three of them.

He stood at least five feet eleven inches tall and because she only stood five feet three he towered over her. She liked.

"......I want to get next to you" she sang.

The classic Rolls Royce song from the soundtrack of that 70's movie played over the elevator speaker. She remembered a pretty waitress at a diner in pink and a guy with a huge afro sitting on a swivel chair at a counter. The man was interested in the waitress but the waitress showed no interest in him at all.

"What was the name of that movie" she questioned herself aloud.

"Car Wash I believe" he answered.

"That's right, it was. A bunch of guys running around all day doing everything but what they were being paid to do" Gigi exclaimed. "I loved that movie. It was the funniest movie about absolutely nothing."

"I agree" chuckled the handsome stranger, "I believe my mother wore that soundtrack album out!!"

"My big sister did, too. Do you remember the scene with Richard Pryor as Big Daddy Rich and the hooker gave him some change as an offering because he agreed to help find the trick she fell in love with? That face when he dropped it into the car was classic." laughed Gigi. "And the Native American with the pig ears was pretty funny too. My name is Anjelica by the way" she said while laughing and extended her hand "but everybody calls me Gigi."

"Are you freaking kidding me" he marveled.

"I'm sorry, did I say something wrong?"

"You can't be serious" he fumed and ripped off his hat.

"Chance" she gasped, "what on earth are you doing here?"

"Taking my black ass to work just like you. He was livid. How could he have done all of those nasty things to her so many nights and she not know him?

"But you don't work anywhere near here, how was I supposed to know you were you? I'm sorry, Chance, let me make it up to you. Would you like to grab a cup of coffee sometime or maybe lunch?"

I'm sorry but I'm going to have to take a rain check, prior engagement, you know how that is. Perhaps another time, okay? Try to stay warm, I'll see you later" he said.

He winked his eye and walked off towards Ontario Street. He didn't feel bad about the egg she wore on her face and he turned back to sear the look into his memory. She was so beautiful, so sexy. He refused to leave her like that and apologetically walked back to the elevator doors and stepped inside.

"Fuck coffee and lunch, how about some sausage for breakfast" he asked with a naughty grin and closed the elevator doors.

He pressed the stop button then lifted her from the ground and tongue kissed her. He immersed himself in her scent and devoured her neck pressing her back against the glass wall window. He put her down and turned her to face the world below them and raised her coat and dress.

"Just as I thought, your nasty ass ain't wearing no gotdamn panties" he murmured in her ear.

His dick slid into her with relative ease and he propelled into her with two strong pumps that made her cry out into the silence of the parking garage elevator, stopped and locked on the 7th floor. He pulled out of her and powerfully jammed back into her with an immeasurable force and just as forcefully pulled back out. He slapped her ass, straightened up and fastened his pants.

"You know where to find me if you want more of that" he said and smiled.

"Are you for real? You're just going to tease me like that and then walk away just like that" she asked with attitude.

"Yup, just like that. Bye." he said as the elevator doors opened. "This is where I get off."

She was dazed. She couldn't remember the last time a man slid into her pussy and pulled out before he came if there ever was a time like that. He had some good dick but not all that good to walk away from here like that. This was an unfamiliar feeling and she didn't like it. Damn tease.

She smoothed her dress and coat down then reached into her bag and retrieved a decorative silk scarf. She tied it around her neck, gathered her coat, and went out into the sharp, morning cold. She froze in her tracks when she realized he'd entered her without a condom. Bastard. He knew that shit was against her rules.

She walked hurriedly to the office, spoke to the receptionists and made her way to her desk. Her best friend and assistant Sydney had arrived before her this morning and greeted her with a hearty "Good morning".

"Oh my God, that cold out there is downright disrespectful. All I want to know is why is it this cold this early? It's just mid-November for crying out loud" she proclaimed to Sydney as she peeled off her coat and scarf.

"I get it, it's Cleveland and you know what they say about the weather here: Cleveland has four-seasons June, July, August and winter but damn this is ridiculous."

Sydney threw her head back and laughed at the joke. She sat at the work station outside of Gigi's office where she'd sat as her assistant for seven years. They met fifteen years prior when Gigi first started working at Glass Slipper Media and watched each other's children grow up, go off to college and the military, marry and now beginning to have children of their own. Gigi was more to Sydney than just her boss. They were the very best of friends.

"Girl!! Let me tell you! I saw Chance in the parking garage" Gigi gushed. "I been toying with the idea of giving him some ever since I saw him at the bar the other week but he just pissed me off and messed that all up. His big ass teased me with a few little pumps of dick just now then hustled his tail out of the damn elevator."

"You bullshitting me. Are you for real" Sydney asked as she hurried into Gigi's office. "So you just gone lay Jesus off to the side like that and go all rogue whore on me?"

"Lay Jesus off to the side? What the hell you talking about? Don't get it twisted dear," Gigi said, "ain't nobody pushing Jesus off nowhere. I'm a woman, I have needs and He understand and yes honey, he will be getting more than a little taste of this if his ass act right."

"Not Ms. Celibate-because-I'm-waiting-on-Jesus talking about a straight booty call but okay, I guess, Church Girl" said Sydney on her way back to her desk.

"Since we're getting all progressive and loose and everything I really wish you would relax a little and let me introduce you to Orlando. He's a good guy Gee, you'd like him."

"You know I don't swirl. Not my thing." Gigi crinkled her nose and continued, "and you know damn well I like chocolate milk. No offense."

"Girl please, I've know you way too long to pay attention to your stupid self. I know you date black dudes exclusively but I still say you'll like him" answered Sydney. "And what do you mean you saw Chance at the bar the other week? What bar and how do you go for weeks and months without seeing him and now you've seen him twice in how many weeks?"

"Girl bye, me and Chance had been hooking up about 3 times a week before he saw me with Oshen that night, what are you talking about" Gigi said and waved her hand in the air.

She made her coffee, opened her sausage and cheese sesame seed bagel, no egg, and then settled in for a long morning. She prepared for her standing Monday morning Team meeting, crunched some numbers with Charla and was exhausted by noon.

She was ready for a change in her boring life. For years, she came into the same door at work, hung her coat on the same hook and ate the same sesame seed bagel with sausage and cheese, no egg. From time to time her boss Charla purchased breakfast but the creature of habit still chose a bagel with sausage and cheese, no egg. The only variance might have been the type of bagel she chose.

Her life was mundane and uneventful with the exception of the occasional hook-up every once and again. Chance and Oshen both were nothing more than hookups to her. Her ex-husband proved to her that men were liars, cheaters and master manipulators and she no longer trusted them. She would never give her heart to another one for as long as she lived although she had no problem with letting them pleasure her when she needed it. They would just never be more to her than that.

"Gigi!" called Erica when she passed by the reception area. "This box came for you and you've gotten at least three roses from Evan Beauchamp. They've come at the top of each hour" she said and handed her the box to Gigi.

"Bitch, you're holding out" said Sydney when Gigi returned to her office. "You fucked him, didn't you?"

"Okay, see now you're seriously bugging. I told you everything that happened with that idiot" she replied.

"Then why is he sending you flowers and gifts and shit" inquired Sydney. "Men send flowers and gifts for two reasons: either they're trying to get some or they already got it."

"Well that's a double negative."

"Lie again, I dare you" Sydney said and they both erupted into laughter.

"What's for lunch" asked Gigi.

"Hell bitch, whatever the hell you brought. Ain't no damn body spending out to eat money with your ass every damn day. Some people got bills and shit to pay." Sydney snapped.

"What I meant was, what did AB have delivered today, and why you got to call people bitches all the time? That's some uncouth behavior right there Sydney" she said.

"Because that's who the fuck I am and that's what the fuck I do. Now, bitch."

"I'm serious Syd, I'm having you committed. You got issues, lady" giggled Gigi as she waved her hand.

That was the one thing about Sydney she disapproved of: her filthy, foul mouth. All of the cussing she did was absurd.

Gigi went into her office, sat in her chair and leaned back. This was the first time she was able to have a moment to herself since she got there this morning. She welcomed the breather although it was lunchtime and she really needed some food in her life.

"Let's go to Lola's, my treat" she called to Sydney. "If we're lucky Michael Symon might be in the house." she said.

She wanted a Muffaletta sandwich from there. She could only eat half of it because it contained so much meat but it was divine.

She sat upright and read the cards tied to each of the roses she got from Evan. The first card read "I'm sorry." The second card read "I'm very sorry." The third card read "I'm very, very sorry." Gigi got the symbolism but Gigi didn't get Evan. She didn't doubt the gift box was also an apology of some sort that she didn't want and grabbed the box and took it to Erica. She wished he'd just go away.

"Whatever's in there you can have because I've had about enough apologies from that imbecile for today" Gigi said and headed back down the hall. She scurried into her office to catch the ringing phone.

"Anjelica Haralson" she answered in her professional work voice. There was no response. "Anjelica Haralson" repeated Gigi.

"Gee" asked the caller.

"Yes, who's this" she asked. "Lena?"

The voice sounded like her cousin but she couldn't really make out who it was for sure.

"No, bitch!" the male voice cackled wickedly, "black ass, fat ass bitch! I'm coming for your black ass" he said.

"Bring your gotdamn ass on then" she yelled before the caller was gone.

She slammed the phone back into its cradle and made a beeline to the front desk. She had to see the caller id to determine who just made that disturbing call.

Erica's bloodcurdling scream stopped her in her tracks as it rang through the office. Gigi, Charla, Sydney and even Dionne ran top speed to the front desk to find Erica trembling in a corner, holding her left hand over her mouth and pointed to the box on the reception desk.

Charla tipped up to the box and peeked over the side to find a dead white dove with dagger piercing its breast. She slowly turned and looked at Gigi.

"Some damn body wanna tell me what the fuck is going on around here?"

Tuesday December 22, 2014: 7:30 a.m.

Gigi's mind drifted to Oshen while she listened to The Tom Joyner Morning Show™ on her way to work the next morning. She knew he would be no more than a screw buddy but *he* had high hopes of them actually being together.

He was too young for her to take him seriously. She wasn't interested in the drama a young man brought to the table: the staying out late, the multiple women. It was just easier to screw him and be done. After all, wasn't that the main reason older people found themselves with younger people anyway?

She dreaded getting out of the car and making that long, cold trek to the office. This morning was one of those mornings when she wished she would have worked remotely. It was undeniably winter so now the ugly winter chukka boots were okay although they were a fashion no-no. Those things were big and clunky and she felt like a lumberjack in them. The cute boots would have a girl with cold, wet feet, staring up at the sky, from the ground so the ugly boots won.

Gigi walked quickly through the parking deck to the elevator. She wouldn't have been able to do that in her cute boots, that's for sure. The elevator doors opened just as she arrived and there he was again.

"Well Good Morning, Beautiful long time, no see" Chance greeted.

"I just saw you a few weeks ago when you teased me with your little dick then bounced, remember" she responded.

He stared at her blankly and shrugged his shoulders. So he toyed with her a little bit, what did she want him to do?

"Let's get one thing straight: my dick is not now nor has it ever been little, Sweet thing" he said and winked his eye.

"Whatever. How you liking this snow?" she asked him, trying to change the conversation.

"I actually prefer the snow, believe it or not. It's the heat I can't stand." he said.

"Well you can have it. My daughter will be all grown up in two more years and I promise you, the day after her eighteenth birthday, this snowbird is getting the hell up out of here. I'm out" giggled Gigi and flashed him the peace sign.

"So, have you thought about a day and time for me to cash in my rain check for that coffee" she asked and coquettishly batted her long eyelashes which made Chase blush and smile.

"Why don't I call you tonight and we can talk about having that hot slippery coffee. You know you been holding out and you know I'm due. I got a whole lot built up and waiting for you, Girl" he replied as he stepped closer to her and pulled her to him.

"Promise you'll call" Gigi pouted.

"I said I would call you didn't I" he asked and kissed her.

"Yes and I'm looking forward to it, Love. Have an awesome day" she said as she watched him walk away.

He reminded her of President Obama when he walked with his confident swagger and debonair assuredness that made her melt. His sex appeal was on 10 today and she eagerly anticipated connecting with him.

She walked quickly to the office through the crisp morning air. Today promised to be a busy day for Gigi. Her department was responsible not only for scheduling live performance tours and booking talent but also for marketing the performances in each city.

There was more radio time she had to purchase as well as additional ads in larger print publications and on large websites. She often solicited students to post fliers on college campuses in exchange for a pair of free tickets to the concert.

She always used free resources as much as possible and placed ads in free or inexpensive digital and print publications.

Charla normally required a member of the GSM Team to go to the venue ahead of the scheduled performance and make sure everything was in order. Thank goodness that wasn't Gigi's department or else she'd be stuck alone with Foolio as she liked to refer to Evan. The moniker was a play on the name of the 90's rapper Coolio and she smiled to herself.

"The For Lovers Only Tour" was to kick-off on New Year's Day January 1 in Las Vegas and wrap up on June 21 some twenty-five weeks and forty performances later in Philadelphia. Tickets went on sale immediately after the Tour was announced in early September and sales were incredible.

The Vegas show was sold out as was Denver, Baltimore, Cleveland, Columbus and the Valentine's Day performance in Chicago.

She planned to spend the day blogging, Face-booking and Tweeting about the old school R&B tour. She also planned to reach out to the urban and R&B radio stations in Las Vegas and the other tour date markets and create last minute promotional giveaways. It was shaping up to be an extremely long and exhausting day.

Her cell phone rang and it was Oshen. She wasn't ready to talk to him and let the call go to straight to voicemail.

She'd made several mistakes with him including the big one she'd made last night by sleeping the entire night in his arms, *if* you could call what they did sleep.

One could set their watch according to his erections and the way he would wake her up by poking her in the rear with his dick or by climbing on top of her. He would gently clean her first with a warm cloth before pleasuring her orally, then proceed to screw the living daylight out of her. She was exhausted and would continue to be if she kept letting this young boy turn her out the way he was.

She felt a bit guilty for sleeping with Oshen last night and making plans to get with Chance today. She questioned if entertaining more than one man sexually was a form of misandry. It wasn't a matter of hating men, she concluded. She didn't trust them and couldn't give all of herself to just one.

She wondered if she could love Oshen. He was a really remarkable man but he was a baby to her, well, except his dick but other than that, he was extra-ordinary when it came to men.

The age difference was crucial to her. She didn't want to be labeled a cougar. Then again, she didn't want to lose the one she knew loved her because of the crap the one who didn't did.

Her thoughts were interrupted by gum-cracking ghetto-fied Dionne. She could never come in quietly without a huge production and it got on Gigi's nerves. Thank God she didn't report to her or that woman would have been gone long ago.

"Hey Girl, where's your girl? I heard she got knocked straight the fuck out" Dionne said as and popped her head into Gigi's office.

"Dionne, what *are* you talking about" asked Gigi.

"I'm talking about your girl, Sydney. I guess that smart ass mouth sold a wolf ticket somebody finally bought" Dionne said and giggled off down the hallway.

"What is the village idiot talking about", Gigi thought to herself and picked up the phone and dialed Sydney.

"Hello" Sydney answered.

"What's this I hear about you getting knocked out and why didn't I hear it from you?"

"Because I didn't get knocked out and it ain't shit."

"Are you coming in? I have a whole lot for you to do today."

"So much for being concerned about a bitch. I'll be there in a few minutes" said Sydney and disconnected the call.

"Fix it, Jesus 'because I can't and I ain't" Gigi said out loud.

She didn't have time for drama today. Tomorrow she would work from Oshen's home office. There was no drama at his place *that* was for sure.

The final draft of the sixty-second promotional spots were ready for legal review and would begin airing across the country once reviewed and approved. Similar spots without Black Ice being mentioned were already playing since they were such a late addition.

Gigi was on a roll today, knocking out a multitude of items on her "to-do" list before noon. Next up was to schedule regular posts to social media accounts on Facebook, Twitter and Instagram was next.

When Sydney arrived, she'd have her schedule the posts for the next 60 days of so. Time was moving rapidly and the kickoff date was fast approaching.

Sydney slipped into the office uncharacteristically quiet. She and Gigi hadn't gotten a chance to talk but Syd was obviously pre-occupied with something. She decided not to pry knowing Syd would talk when she was ready.

"Gigi, Charla wants you in her office" Erica said over the intercom.

"Thanks Erica, I'm on my way."

She grabbed a pad and pen and headed down the hall. She walked into Charla's office and closed the door and her boss wasted no time getting to the point.

"I need you in Vegas on opening night. Actually, I need you there a few days before so prepare to spend New Year's Eve in the great ole state of Nevada" said Charla.

Gigi cringed. That wasn't even her department. She had no desire to be that far away from home by herself on New Year's Eve, and she damn sure didn't want to be *anywhere* near Evan Beauchamp inany capa at all. She was supposed to move that weekend, too.

Why was *she* being sent there anyway? Booking and marketing was not her forte. Normally, logistics like sound, lighting, stuff like that was the venue's responsibility. A technician would be on hand to handle that so she couldn't imagine what purpose her presence would serve, simply couldn't figure it out.

The lunch hour was approaching and Gigi still hadn't spoken with Syd. That girl was never quiet, never at a loss for words but today she was so quiet you could hear your own hair growing.

"Sydney" called Erica over the intercom, "were you expecting Al Bernard? He's here to see you but he's not on anyone's appointment schedule today."

"Will you kindly escort him to the Conference room and block its usage off for the next ninety minutes? Thanks Erica" responded Sydney.

So much for lunch Gigi thought to herself. There was definitely something going on with her friend and she *had* to find out what it was.

"Syd, can I see you a minute" asked Gigi.

"What's up, boo" Sydney said and popped her head into Gigi's office.

"Come in, close the door. What's going on with you, Chicca? I've never seen you melancholy like this in all the years I've known you. What's up?" She motioned for Sydney to sit down.

Sydney stared blankly into her hands for a few moments before slowly lifting her head. She looked at Gigi through bloodshot eyes and fought to hold back tears.

"Can we talk about it later" she asked. "I promise I'll tell you everything, okay" Gigi nodded her head.

"Let me go talk to him for a minute. Your life is not the only life that's changing around here" she said and strolled off to meet with Al Bernard.

Gigi had no clue what that meant. It could mean anything with Sydney though.

She saw that her very fair-skinned sister had some reddening under her bottom lip and chin but no bruises on her face nor were her eyes black. Dionne's assertion that Syd had gotten "knocked out" was erroneous as were most of the things that came out of her mouth. There was a reason no one has ever taken that girl seriously and no one ever would.

Alfred Bernard sat across the conference table from Sydney Zanchak-Taylor. Less than twelve hours before, he had her spread across his dining room table like a Thanksgiving buffet. He feasted on every part of her and used every food item he could think of to do it with.

He'd made a human ice cream sundae out of her by placing scoops of ice cream, caramel and hot fudge down her naked midline and ate it off. He'd drizzled strawberry sauce on her nipples and licked them clean and inserted a peeled banana inside of her and eaten it out.

He'd been banging her so fast and so hard that the $7,000-dollar solid oak table he was doing her on walked across the dining room floor. They changed locations and switched to the floor once AB noticed the table was on a collision course with his priceless china cabinet.

His mother had given him the cabinet when he first purchased the home a few years back. With her passing a few years ago, everything related to her was priceless to him.

"Thanks for seeing me today, Al. Is it okay if I call you that" Sydney asked.

"After last night, Daddy is more appropriate, don't you think" he said with a knowing grin. She shook her head and rolled her eyes upwards.

"Look, I called you here to discuss what happened between us. AB, it was a mistake in so many ways. I'm a married woman, not as happily as I thought but married nonetheless. You're married too and to top it all off, you're a client. You and I cannot happen, we cannot be friends with benefits or fuck buddies and booty calls, or whatever you wanna call them cannot happen between you and me, ever."

He sat silently and listened to her speak. Women say the dumbest things out of their mouths. He had every intention of hitting that on the regular regardless of what she was talking about.

"Al? Are you listening to me?"

"I hear you, Baby. I heard every word you said and now it's my turn."

He walked over and sat on the table in front of her and peered into her dark eyes. He opened his mouth to speak but instead leaned in and kissed her. With all the big bad Syd talk, she melted when he touched her. She was soft and pliable under his caress, no matter how many asses she threatened to kick. Sydney was the Abominable Snowman with no teeth: roar for days and not a single bite. He took her hand and kissed it.

"Meet me tonight. There's a wonderful little vineyard in Canton I think you'll love. They've got a Meatball Spiedini to die for and a Pesto Chicken you'll beat somebody's mama down over. You can leave your car at my house and we'll just go have a good time. How's that sound?"

"I'm going to have to pass. You're a good guy but what happened between us cannot and will not happen again. Now if you'll excuse me, I've got to get back to work. Have a good day" she said she with authority and extended her hand.

"Girl, you out your gotdamn mind. Get your ass over here" he said and drew her into his chest.

He looked down into her eyes and saw a sadness he wanted to take away. He had to finesse this woman away from her so-called husband. It was obvious he hadn't been treating her right.

"You may be married to him; you may love him but you want me. Tell me I'm wrong and I'll walk away from you right now and you'll never see me outside of work again but if I'm right, be at my place at 9 o'clock better yet, make it 7 o'clock." He turned to leave then continued, "and by the way I've been divorced for 3 years, I ain't married. I'll see you at 7" he said and winked before disappearing out of sight.

Sydney blushed and shuddered. She had to admit he wasn't too hard on the eyes and comely to say the least, but she already had a husband. She'd crossed the line last night. He wasn't married but she was and no matter what Tim did and who he did it with, she couldn't repay his evil with her own. She definitely would not be meeting Al Bernard tonight or any other night.

"Hey Girl. I see you over there creeping, hunh? I know miss happily married for 17 years ain't stepping out on that fine ass man you got" purred Dionne and stepped dangerously into Sydney's personal space.

"Don't leave the door open because a bitch like me will have no problem walking right on in" she whispered into Sydney's ear.

"And a bitch like me don't have a problem fucking a bitch like you the fuck up if a bitch like you do. Nice having this little chat" Syd said.

"Wonderful chat, white girl. You might wanna switch it back up though, Sydney Zanchak. That wannabe black girl routine is a bit tired, don't 'cha think" asked Dionne snidely.

"Bitch, you stole that shit from Beauty Shop. Bye, Felicia" she yelled at Dionne as she strutted away.

Sydney shook her head at herself. She accused Dionne's stupid butt of stealing a line from Beauty Shop and she responds to a stolen line *with* a stolen line from Friday. Maybe Gigi *was* right. Maybe she *was* crazy. Sydney laughed at herself and walked back to her desk.

She may have been done with the issue but Dionne could not wait to get back to her desk and share the titbit of information she heard and saw today between Sydney and AB.

"I just heard your bitch hooking up with dude tonight. Told you that white bitch was scandalous" Dionne texted.

Truth be told, Dionne didn't truly want to be with Tim. He was a liar and a cheater for god sake. She simply loved sticking it to Sydney. Sydney thinks she's a dumb, low budget whore, well Sydney Zanchak-Taylor's world was about to come crashing down at the hands of the low budget whore. Dionne was telling and she was telling it all.

"What dude? And I've told you about your mouth when it comes to my wife. You're my bitch, she's my wife, don't ever forget that shit. What motherfucking dude are you talking about?" texted Tim.

"Fuck you, motherfucker, I ain't telling your ass shit, talking to me any kind of damn way" texted Dionne. She had information he needed not the other way around.

"I'll be there by 7 o'clock and that ass better be butt ass naked and ready to tell me what the fuck I want to know. You understand that shit" texted Tim.

"What the fuck ever" texted Dionne.

Tim wasn't her man and never would be but Dionne had never been one to pass up some good dick. Little did his dumb ass know, his bitch would be getting it in with AB by 7 o'clock while he's crawling up in between her legs. Silly ass men, always trying to get theirs and oblivious to the fact that their woman is somewhere getting hers.

She hopped in the shower and pampered her pussy with Island Splash cleansing gel and douched with her favorite Island Splash both by Summer's Eve™. She always took whatever solution remained in the douche bottle and cleaned her anus. She couldn't get a wash cloth up that far after all plus, Tim loved to toss her salad so the salad bowl needed to be sparkling clean.

Dionne giggled to herself. Bye Felicia, indeed. That's why Felicia fucking your man. Bitch.

Chapter 7

Jingle All the Way

Monday December 22, 2014

It was the Holiday season in the city of Cleveland and Christmas was just days away. Gigi had been at Oshen's place for close to seven weeks and it was time for her to move on. He'd become a little too comfortable with her around evidenced by little things like walking into her room without knocking, kissing her at will, questioning her whereabouts and the like.

The condo sold in what Gigi considered record time so she sought residency at several apartment complexes all of which accepted her application. She was still in the market for a new house though and had plans to continue working with Brenda to nab something cheap and inexpensive off of the foreclosure market. A short sale would be awesome.

She and Oshen were meeting up for dinner at Red in Beachwood after work. That was as good a time as any to tell him she was moving.

"Hey there, Beautiful" he said as he stood to greet her.

He pulled out her chair and kissed her hand in true gentlemanly fashion. He was a true gentleman, that fact could never be denied.

He'd ordered her a small salad and a Pomegranate Martini while waiting for her to arrive. Red had only two appetizers that didn't contain seafood but French onion soup and or Stuffed Hot Peppers didn't sound appetizing at this late hour. She hated seafood and she was quietly impressed that he remembered that.

"I've found an apartment and it'll be ready on the 1st so I'll be moving the first weekend in January…well make that the 2nd weekend if that's okay. I've got to go out of town for work the 1st but I don't want to impose any more than I have to" she told him.

"Stop it, you know you're not imposing" he said.

"I just want you to be able to get back to your normal life with me and my drama out of your hair. I know I'm a whole lot" she added.

He didn't respond. He was a thousand miles away in his head, pondering returning to a life without her. He'd grown use to her and the smells coming out of the kitchen when she cooked. He liked hearing her pull into the driveway and seeing her little size 7 Louis boots at the back door next to his size 13 Timberland boots. He was used to her coat in the closet next to his. He loved everything about her and he didn't want her to leave.

After dinner, Oshen followed Gigi back to his house. Most of the houses in the neighborhood were all decked out with holiday lights and she was giddy with excitement. She reminded him of a little kid the way she oooed and aahed over the lights as she talked to him on her Bluetooth. The small act endeared her to him even more and that's when it hit him: he had fallen in love with her and could not let her leave.

They arrived at the house after dinner and Gigi went to her bathroom to take a shower. She loved the way the hot water felt as it flowed down her body. The water relaxed her and took her to far off places in her head as all of the day's tension washed down the drain. She lathered up with her favorite shower gel and washed every square inch of her body, giving most of her attention to the golden nugget nestled between her legs.

She may have been horny as hell since her sexual savage had been awakened but she was no stranger to hitting herself in the shower. After bringing herself to climax under the power of the jets on the showerhead, she grabbed a big fluffy towel and sat on the guest bed to dry off.

"Come on in, O" she called upon hearing him knock at the bedroom door. That was unusual for him. He stopped knocking weeks ago.

"What's up, sweetie" she asked.

"I've got a few things I want to say and I don't want you to interrupt me until I'm finished, agreed" he asked.

"Agreed" she answered.

She was confused. They'd just spent hours talking over dinner. What else could he still have to talk about tonight?

"Gigi when I wake in the morning, I think of you and when I fall asleep at night, I fall asleep thinking of you. You invade my daydreams and possess my dreams at night. When I'm working and I'm on that field, I'm trying my damndest to reach the end zone for you, to make you proud of me. Well, my Mother too but you get the gist of what I'm saying.

From the moment I saw you in the parking lot running from that clown, I've wanted nothing more than to make you mine. Anjelica, I don't want you to move out. Baby I'm begging you to stay here with me, *please*. I need you."

He gazed up at her kneeling on the floor, holding her hands in his. He wanted her to say something, anything to assure him he didn't just make a fool of himself but she didn't speak. This much younger, much richer man was at her feet begging her to be his and she was mystified.

"Baby, don't leave me out here like this, say something, anything" he pleaded with her.

"What about Bambi? How can you be here asking me to allow you into my bed and my heart when you have someone, Oshen. I'm too old to play damn games."

"Bambi? You men the PFL jump off? *That* whore? Baby girl, that woman is *not* my girl. I've never even touched her! Wait. Did she approach you like she was mine" he questioned.

"Why would I ask if she hadn't."

"That chic is delusional. I am not now nor have I ever been interested in Bambi Dough. That woman has been passed around by so many players on so many teams, it's unbelievable. I guess she's got *me* in her sights now, huh" he asked.

He got up and paced the floor. He stopped in mid-pace and seductively stared at the towel clad Gigi, water droplets still meandering down her body.

"Have you seen me with any other women besides you, anyone at all?"

She shook her head and he knelt back down at her feet. He had this thing about making her feel comfortable and safe when she was with him. He loomed over her at 6 feet tall which always gave him the power advantage. Kneeling transferred it to her.

"Oshen how do I look tangling myself up with a man twelve years my junior? You're a baby to me! What happens when you want a baby? Hell at my age, I don't want any more babies, all of my kids are grown and gone, except Rain of course but what happens when you start thinking about your legacy and leaving heirs and all that stuff men think about when it comes to kids. See, the idea of us is cute to you now that you're thirty-two years old and I'm forty-five, but will it still be cute when you're a mere fifty and I'm sixty-three freaking years old? You're a professional athlete, Oshen, a big, solid, professional and rich, football player of all things. These thirsty broads out here *throwing* pussy at you, I've seen them with my own eyes. You're a man, Baby. I would be playing myself to think that you won't eventually catch what these heffas are out here throwing, I'm not delusional, O! The waitress tonight for example, where did she write her telephone number for you, on a napkin or the receipt?"

"Baby I'm not going to lie, she wrote it on the back of the receipt but I don't want her, all I want is you. Gigi, let me protect you, celebrate you, provide for you. Let me love you damn, all I need is a chance, Baby. That's all I'm asking for is a chance. Let me prove to you I'm not like these other dudes out here" he said.

He reached up and loosened her towel letting it topple to the ground, freeing her breasts. He reached up and cupped a breast in each hand and she leaned her head back and moaned when he squeezed and sucked her nipples, alternating between one and then the other.

"I swear I'll be good to you" he said between sucks.

He reached around behind her, grabbed her by her hair and bent her head back to kiss her. He kissed every square inch of her neck, then kissed his way down her chest back down to her nipples where he took one into his mouth and rolled the free one between his thumb and forefinger.

Gigi whined and squealed and twisted under his touch. She thought she might explode and lose her substance before he even entered her. He hadn't even touched her genitals yet. What was she going to do then?

"Maybe we shouldn't do this, Oshen" she sighed.

"Relax. Tell me it doesn't feel right and I'll stop."

He waited for her response and after hearing none he released her breast and kissed his way down her middle. He skipped over her throbbing pussy and kissed the inside of her thigh.

"You'll never want for another thing another day in your life" he whispered and nibbled his way up the inside of her other thigh.

He blew on her clean shaven pussy on the way down, teasing her aching clit with the sensation and she rounded her back towards his face.

He changed directions and flicked his tongue against the tip of her clit, then planted light kisses back up the middle of her stomach, between her breasts, her neck and finally found her lips.

His thick tongue found its way into her mouth and he zealously kissed her. He kissed her so long and so deep that she couldn't remember where he began and she ended. Their bodies were pressed very tightly together and she didn't know if she was feeling his heartbeat or her own.

Oshen gently laid her back onto the bed, careful not to lay his weight on top of her or allow his bulging, throbbing dick to rub against her. He showcased his youthful athleticism and balanced himself on his hands, hovering above her and he intensely kissed her. No part of their bodies touched except their lips but every nerve in her body was on fire.

He broke the long, lingering kiss and led her by the hand to *his* bedroom, to *his* bed. A woman had never lain in his bed before and this was special to him. She was his chosen one and for the first time in his life he was going to take a woman in his own bed. Mayven had never had the pleasure of enjoying his PFL money as she had gotten pregnant and gave Evan a child before all of his riches and success really settled in. Gigi was more special to him than she realized.

He rested her on top of the juicy comforter to take in every plus sized inch of her. She was stunningly beautiful to him and he was absolutely in love with her. Oshen returned her to her feet and searched her eyes, hoping for some sign that she loved him too.

"I swear I won't hurt you, Anjelica. I love you, Girl. Trust me. Do you trust me?" he asked her.

"Oshen, I..." she started to answer but he sucked her tongue into his mouth before she could finish.

He lifted her up against the wall and she placed her legs over his shoulders. Their eyes locked and they both understood what he had planned for her.

He took a minute to revere her pretty pussy. It was perfect and he sucked the lips into his mouth, elongated them away from her body and repeated the act again. His flat tongue moved across the surface area of her pussy before he inserted it into her and repeatedly fucked her.

He was driving her insane and she was fast losing control. She'd been backed across a bed before but that was nothing compared to what Oshen was doing to her. She grabbed her breasts and squeezed them and grinded into his face, moving in rhythm with his tongue. Finally, the walls of her pussy began to contract wildly and violently. He felt her body shaking with orgasmic pleasure and continued his oral assault.

"Damn! Oo-shshsh-ennnn!! Shiittttt" she screamed when she came. He continued to suck her, allowing her crisis to ooze all over his face. When he finally let her down from the wall he licked her lips and kissed her.

"You taste your pussy, Baby? You smell you on my lips" he asked her.

She licked his lips and smiled and then she inserted her finger into her pussy, sucked it and shared her juice with him.

She kissed all over his neck and his chest, stopping to play with his nipples. She teased them and nipped them and traced tiny figure eights around them with her tongue as he moaned aloud before she dropped to her knees.

She took his balls in her hand and jiggled them like a pair of dice while teasing the head of his dick like she was licking a lollipop.

She then deliberately took him into her mouth, an inch at a time until he began to hit the back of her throat. She salivated irrepressibly and uncompromisingly when he pleasured himself in her mouth in cadence with the tick-tock of the antique Grandfather clock that stood in the corner of the spacious room. She responded to his movements and tightened her mouth around his member each time he withdrew from her mouth and jostled his balls every time he entered.

Thick white saliva dripped from her mouth onto his balls and the sight of it increased his dick's rigor. He was hard enough to plow a hole into concrete and eager to enter her but she wasn't finished. Not yet.

She popped him out of her mouth and sucked the saliva off of his balls, one at a time, moaning as she did so and he felt a huge nut build up.

"Damn, Girl" Oshen shouted and shot his load down her throat. He gripped her head and held it in place and she continued to suck until his balls were dry.

They both were weak when he helped her off of the floor to her feet and they collapsed onto his bed...or so she thought.

"Oh, you think I'm finished. Well, I ain't no 50-year-old, baby we can do this shit all night if you want to" he said with his mouthful of her tit.

Her bullet sized nipple glistened when he loosened his grip and let it fall out of his mouth. She moaned with pleasure and he realized that was her sweet spot. He took his hands and pushed both breasts together, devouring them simultaneously and she moaned and thrashed under his touch. He parted her legs and climbed in between them, rubbing his stiff dick against her still enflamed clit.

"Not without a condom you're not" she said and sent him to retrieve one from the cabinet in his bathroom.

"You do it for me" he said and handed it to her.

She opened the Magnum™ brand condom and rolled it down onto his thick appendage. He placed one of her legs over his shoulder and she wrapped the other around his waist.

Oshen turned his face and licked her leg from her inner knee down to her ankle and she spread her legs even wider and grabbed his dick to guide him into her.

He entered her with ease and packed her pussy chock-full of his rock hard dick. He took his time with her and slowly grinded inside of her then switched cadence and abruptly pounded into her like his life depended on it. Her pussy felt like warm, wet silk to him as her walls gripped him with every plunge.

"Get on top," he told her "ride me, Baby."

Oshen lay flat on his back as Gigi lowered herself onto his upright dick.

"Unh..." she said aloud as he filled her up. "Shit!"

She placed both of her hands on his chiseled pecs and rode him like a bull in a rodeo. She moved her hips like she'd seen the riders do so many times before on TV only she wouldn't let *him* throw her off. He placed his hands around her waist and moved with her, feeling her clit rubbing against his pubic bone. She leaned forward and he began to rhythmically pommel her hard and fast, slapping their bodies together like a thunderous round of applause.

"Damn" Oshen exclaimed, "here it comes! I love you, Gigi! I love you, Baby" he wailed and climaxed.

Her eyes popped wide open and she looked down at him confused. He couldn't possibly love her could he? This little boy didn't even know her and it's on been a few weeks. Love doesn't happen instantly, that takes time and that's why she didn't mess with kids.

"Oh my god" she thought to herself, "what in the hell did I just do?"

Chapter 8

Secret Lovers

Monday December 29, 2014: 5:20 p.m.

In the car, Chance? In the gotdamn car" she asked while he sucked on her nipples and worked his hand inside of her pants. "We ain't teenagers no more, you know."

"Shut up, Damn" he said and showered her with kisses.

"I knew your horny ass ain't have no under wear, I knew that shit" he said and grabbed a handful of her smooth pussy. He gently placed two fingers inside of her and played inside of her with them until she begged him to enter her.

"You want some dick" he asked her and removed his fingers, "then you and that fat ass pussy of yours meet me tonight. Don't be late and don't show up driving that motherfucker's car, drive your own shit. That's some fucked up shit right there, Anjelica. How the fuck you try to fuck a man in another man's car? You driving the man's luxury ass ride but he's not your man? Get out of here with that shit. Don't be late Gigi" he said and slammed the car door leaving her alone, half-naked, horny and bothered.

She wondered what all of that was about and fixed her clothing. They had agreed to be friends with benefits until further notice so why was he acting like that? She shook her head, fixed her makeup and drove home wondering why he caught feelings and gotten mad because she hadn't.

She pulled in the driveway and Oshen met her at the garage door. His face looked angry and she wondered what was going on. She knew *she* hadn't done anything to piss him off.

"Hey, what's up? Where you been" Oshen queried. "I've been trying to reach you all day. What's up, you good?"

"Yes, I'm good. It's just been a really long day and it's not done. I have to run out tonight and meet a client for dinner."

"I wish you would have called; I've got dinner going now" he said. She stopped for a moment and contemplated her next words.

"Oshen we have great, no we have explosive sex but explosive sex does not a relationship make. You're not my man and I'm not your woman. I don't owe you phone calls and explanations of my whereabouts. I like you, I really do but explosive sex is all it is, that's all I have to give. I'm not ready for a relationship, not right now, okay?"

"Come here" he responded but she didn't move. "Fine, I'll come to you." He walked over and put his arms around her waist, drawing her to him.

"Anjelica Haralson, I am head over heels in love with you. It ain't just the sex, Baby girl, it's you. I've *never* waited that long to be with a woman, I never had to actually, but you're special and you were worth it. So if you're not ready to be with me like that, that's fine. I'll just wait until you *are* ready, is that cool?"

She looked into his eyes and saw that he really did love her but love wasn't enough. They weren't kids anymore and that feel good, fluffy stuff just wasn't going to be sufficient at her age. There had to be more.

"O, I'm looking for more, a whole lot more. You've shown me that you can protect me and have definitely shown me that you can set my body on fire. You blow my mind sexually and you know that but that's not love, Baby and you haven't shown me much else" she said.

"What else is there" he asked.

"O, do you pray? I mean you talk a lot about protecting me but can you pray and cover me?" She took his face in her hands and continued. "Do you even know what that means? I think we're great friends, that can't be denied, I mean you keep me laughing but O, what are your dreams, what are your plans *after* football? I don't know that about you. If I'm your woman, I need to be able to support you, support your dreams, and push you to be greater. I need to be able to have your back and to understand your vision as you should mine." She kissed him lightly on his lips.

"And your family…what is your mother going to say when you show up with my cougar-ing self? You think she's going to embrace a woman damn near her age pushing up on her baby? That's drama waiting to happen, O. There's a whole lot more to consider when deciding to enter into a relationship with me, a whole hell of a lot more to consider than love." She stood on her tip-toes and kissed him again.

"…and can you be faithful? With all of the beautiful women across the country literally gift-wrapping themselves for you and men like you, can you actually promise me that you can be faithful? That is more important to me than anything else. Think about it." she said. She had to get dressed.
Chance and his beautiful fat friend would be waiting.

8:12 p.m.

Chance checked the time on his wrist watch. She was late and he abhorred tardiness. It was one of the most disrespectful things a person could do to him. His time was just as valuable as hers and he did not take kindly to it being wasted.

He glanced down at the timepiece once again. He loved watches and had an unhealthy obsession with them. He found it sad that not very many people wore them anymore as most people kept time by their cell phones. They even used them to wake them in the morning rather than an actual bedside alarm clock.

Back in his day, people used ridiculously loud Big Ben alarm clocks to jolt them out of their sleep and he still did. The weak beep from a cell phone would never awake him from his slumber. He was like a hibernating bear when he slept and nothing but a loud, blaring Big Ben would ever be a sufficient method for waking him.

He would give her another five minutes and then he would eat the dinner he'd prepared for them by himself. He should have known she wouldn't show; the beautiful people *never* did. They weren't people of integrity like him and the rest of the word and they were all under the impression that the sun rose and set around them. Well *his* world neither rose nor set around Anjelica Haralson, he didn't care how beautiful she was. She was just like the rest of them in his opinion.

He saw her repeatedly with Oshen Benjamin and with Evan Beauchamp probably early November when she swore she was working. Evan looked like he was running behind her as if they were in some sort of argument. Next thing he knew, she left in a car with Benjamin and Beauchamp was left standing there looking stupid. That would never be him. He wasn't running up behind her and nobody else for that matter.

She was a gold-digging woman anyway or worse yet, a media whore. He followed them to the bar that night and by the time he left, there were cameras all outside trying to get a shot. She knew her photograph would be snapped by the paparazzi and plastered all over Facebook, Instagram and Twitter whenever she hung out with the likes of Benjamin and Beauchamp. There was no chance of that happening with him. Absolutely none.

Chance checked his watch one last time. She definitely was a no-show. She was probably somewhere with Oshen riding his pole because she wasn't sleeping at her own place, that's for sure. He'd been by her house a couple times and she was never there. Her truck hadn't moved in weeks but she showed up for work in a brand new Mercedes. He was going to give her a really good piece of his mind and he couldn't wait to see her again.

He blew out the lavender and vanilla scented candles that he knew to be her favorite and turned on the dining room lights. He tossed her plate into the trash without scraping it and threw her wine glass across the room where it smashed into a billion pieces against the wall.

This was the first and last time she would *ever* disrespect his time. He'd guarantee that.

Chapter 9

Change in the Air

Tuesday December 30, 2014: 5:00 a.m.

The sound of the alarm clock screeched in the darkness. Gigi couldn't believe it was five o'clock already. It felt like she'd just collapsed into bed and drifted off into an amazing never land. She extended her hand to press the snooze button and he grabbed it and tenderly placed her fingers to his lips and kissed them.

"Good morning, Bella" he said.

He brushed his tongue across her fingertips with each word he spoke, tracing the whirls of her fingerprints, each one unique and different like her.

His voice was smooth and fluid like silk but deep and rumbling like thunder. Gigi's stomach was always filled with butterflies anytime he addressed her and he spoke with such authority. There was nothing sexier than that.

"Good Morning," she said and turned her head away from him. He gently placed his finger under her chin and turned her face back into his direction. It was 5:00 a.m. and her kick-ass morning breath was in full effect but he didn't care. He wanted to see her eyes dance in the moonlight that shone in threw the bedroom window.

He turned on the bedside lamp and with no words and no warning grabbed her into his arms and kissed her. He sucked her bottom lip, then her top. He discovered her mouth with his tongue, and kissed her again. Long. Fervently. Deep.

His tongue traced circles and waves on her neck and then her shoulders. He found his way to her breasts where her nipples stood tall like mountainous peaks, wanting and needing him to suck them. He cupped both breasts and squeezed them, allowing the overflow to spill threw his fingers.

Gigi closed her eyes and arched her back anticipating the feel of his wet mouth encasing her waiting, erect nipples. She slowly opened her eyes and was met by his amorous, piercing gaze.

"What" she asked, puzzled.

"I don't want to rush. I want to take my time and do it right" he said.

"Oshen you're a tease. I should be mad at you anyway for making me miss my appointment last night, damn you" she said and playfully pounded his chest.

"I have to go to Vegas for a few days for Charla. The tour kicks off on the 1st so I need to be there by tomorrow" she told him.

"So you want me to come with you? My season's done so I've got time." he said.

Oshen suffered a concussion in the 2nd to last game of the season. With the PFL concussion policy, he had to sit out the next game until he was cleared to play by a physician. So for all intent and purposes, his season was done.

"Nah, I should be okay. I'm just going to run by the house and grab a few things. I'll take Sydney with me. You know she thinks she's the female version of Hong Kong Phooey. Mild-mannered Executive Assistant transformed into a super crime-fighting hero by the magic in her filing cabinet!" Gigi responded as she laughed out loud. Hong Kong Phooey was a Saturday morning cartoon that aired in the '70's and parodied popular martial arts films of the decade.

"You're right about that Sydney is indeed a pistol" Oshen chuckled.

"What do you know about Hong Kong Phooey, youngster? It was off the air before you were even born" she teased.

"Cartoon Network. Everything old is new again."

"I've got to get out of here. I've got to pack and be on a plane tomorrow" she said and shook her head.

"Wait a minute, come back here" Oshen said and pulled her back down on the bed. "Is that punk ass Evan going to be out there because I don't want to have to bust him up. He's already put his hands on you twice, are you sure you're going to be all right?"

"O, I've got this okay? Trust me baby" replied Gigi.

"It's not you I don't trust" answered Oshen. "I know how slimy that dude truly is. The two of us already have a serious beef over a woman and I'm telling you right now Gee if that fool touches you one more damn time, it's a rap. Seriously."

"Well since you put it that way, I guess I could think of worse people to spend New Year's Eve with so I guess it's a date. Do I need to bring extra money for bail?"

"As long as that bitch ass motherfucker don't fuck with you, it's all gravy, Baby."

They both laughed out loud at the corny line.

Gigi was bringing Sydney and Tim along for the ride as well. Charla would pay for Syd because she was her assistant but Tim was on his own.

The tension in that marriage was thicker than it'd ever been before. Syd was tired of the openness of their relationship. She was a very outspoken person so it seemed to Gigi that if she'd told *her* she was done with the lifestyle, she'd told *him* as well. Rather than focus his attention on his wife, Tim had taken his outside conquests underground. She hoped they could survive this but she had her doubts.

"Come let me taste some of that honey before you go. Girl, I swear I'm addicted to you" said Oshen.

"I can't, I have to be at work. The great Killer Wave may have a 4-month off season but Anjelica Haralson has to chase this paper" she said and hopped into the shower.

"You ever give Evan some of that" Oshen yelled into the bathroom while reclining across the bed.

"Little boy, ain't nobody got time to play games with you. No, not once, ever and don't ask me again" she yelled back.

"So he just sweating you because you won't let him taste that thang, huh" he asked.

"Is that so hard to believe" she questioned.

"What about old dude at the bar? Now I know you was doing him. He couldn't keep his eyes off you".

"That was the past" she lied, "and why are you asking me all of these questions like you're my man?"

"Because I am" he laughed.

"Boy, bye" she giggled.

"So do I get to meet the parents for Christmas or what" he asked her.

"I would like to plead the 5th if I may, thank you" she said.

"I'm going to my parents' house anyway, how you like that? Wanna come?"

"Oshen, get out, my goodness. Can I *please* enjoy my shower in peace? *Please!*"

1:10 p.m.

C'mon Sydney, we're only going to be a little while, with your scary self" Gigi said after work that day.

Their flight was scheduled to leave in the morning and there were some pieces at her house she wanted to take along. Oshen's stylist was cool but her tastes in jewelry and footwear left much to be desired.

"Just two little seconds, I only want to grab a couple pair of shoes and some boots and a few pieces of jewelry. We'll be in and out, I promise."

Gigi's cellphone rang. She glanced at the display and pressed ignore. The call was coming from an unknown telephone number and she didn't answer unknown calls on her personal cell phone.

"Bitch, are you sure we're going to be all right in this joint? Hell, I'm to the point that I hate to be around your ass. One of these motherfuckers out to get you, for real. Black roses and snakes and shit" Sydney said and surveyed her surroundings.

"Syd?! Please with all the bitches. I hate that in you, for real. Why would you call another female a bitch? Why? That's all I want to know" asked Gigi.

"I call you whatever the fuck you're acting like at that time and right now you acting a little bit like a bitch" said Sydney matter-of-factly.

"Hopeless" said Gigi and bounded up the stairs to her bedroom.

Vongi, her playful Yorkie, was close behind. She loved her little dog. That was literally the only thing that survived her marriage. The fur, the bag, the cheap ring, even the wedding dress all found themselves in the trash can on the curb waiting to be picked up one Thursday morning. Not her baby.

She rambled through her closet searching for her desired pieces. There was no way she was leaving all of her clothes behind. She agreed with Oshen that she wasn't safe and sold the house but he also wanted her to leave everything behind and start completely anew. She'd agreed to leave all of her furnishings but *not* her clothes. She'd spent way too much money on her wardrobe to walk away.

She made a mental note to hire some movers to pack and move her things to her new place while she was out of town. Oshen could kiss her ass when it came to her wardrobe.

"You fuck Oshen yet" Sydney asked.

Gigi almost choked on her own saliva. The woman could be too blunt at times.

"What makes you think I would entertain that young man like that, Sydney? I'm so far out of his league" she answered knowing full well he had been blowing her back out regularly.

"Hell, you let him suck your pussy, I just figured it was only a matter of time before you smashed, that's all."

"Forget my love life, Nosey Rosie, let's talk about yours. Previously on the Syd and Tim show: Syd was tired of Tim's sex-capades and was considering giving Al Bernard a try" she said in a low, hushed announcer's voice. Start talking, sister."

"Okay, all kidding aside, I'm not happy and everything is *not* all right. He's definitely cheating and I don't know what to do about it" said Syd sadly.

Gigi went over to her friend, sat on the bed beside her and took her hand. She intended to comfort and encourage her to pray and heed to the voice of The Lord but Sydney was having none of that.

"...but tell that bitch if I catch her, I'm a beat her ass!"

The two friends fell back on the bed laughing. You could always depend on a one-liner from the movie 'Friday' to lighten any mood. Sydney obviously didn't want to discuss her situation and Gigi quickly changed the subject.

The women were startled out of their skin by what sounded like the front door slamming shut. Vongi heard it too. He jumped off of the bed and took off running and barking down the stairs as if he were chasing a squirrel or a rabbit through the yard.

"Oshen" Gigi called out.

There was no answer. She got up and went to the window to see who was parked in the drive but saw no car other than Oshen's Benz and *she* was driving *it*.

"Brenda" she called to the real estate agent.

Perhaps it was her. Agents sometimes held Open Houses on Sundays but those were always scheduled in advance. Besides that, the sale closed last week. The unit was sold as is with all furniture and decorative items included. Gigi was allowed to remove her personal effects only.

"Syd you did closed the door behind you, didn't you" Gigi asked when Brenda did not answer.

"Don't ask me dumb ass questions, Bitch."

Gigi glared at her and tip-toed to the door. She peered into the hallway to the right and then to the left, and motioned for Sydney to join her. They both removed their stiletto boots and padded down the stairs in their bare feet.

A deep growl penetrated the atmosphere as the huge beast rounded the corner and appeared at the bottom of the winding staircase with a limp Vongi clasped in its jaws.

"Oh shit" the women screamed in concert and retreated back up the stairs with the huge Cane Corso hot on their heels. They ran into Gigi's bedroom and slammed the door shut behind them. The women shrieked as the massive beast rammed the door over and over again. Sydney rushed to Gigi's bed and retrieved a Beretta .357 Stampede from her bag.

"Bitch, move your motherfucking ass" she screamed at Gigi.

She aimed at the door and squeezed the trigger. BOOM! One shot. BOOM! Two shots. The rounds easily penetrated the thin door hitting the massive dog. It yelped out in agony and hit the floor with a loud thud.

They listened at the door as the wounded dog whined and whimpered before deciding it was safe to make a run for the outside door.

The two women joined hands and stepped out of the room. Sydney, who had an affinity for the breed, stopped and reached down to comfort the beast while Gigi found and cradled her Vongi. He too seemed to be critically injured but not dead. Yet.

As they sat on the floor attending to injured dogs, Sydney called the animal hospital and Gigi called the police. Anjelica Haralson studied her friend and realized there was a whole lot about her that she didn't know at all. This white girl was a whole lot more street, more gangster than she realized.

"Syd" she called to her friend.

"What's up" Sydney answered as she held the Cane Corso's paw in her hand.

"Where the fuck did your little ass get a motherfucking Magnum bitch, blowing holes in doors and shit! Now *I* gotta fix that bullshit, damn your ass!"

2:34 p.m.

The Police department arrived and started their investigation taking tons of photos and collecting evidence. There was no doubt that Gigi was being stalked and the Police asked her to construct a list of possible perpetrators.

She briefly considered Chance. He'd popped up out of nowhere a few times within the last month or so and it was beginning to bother her. She never saw him unless it was time for him to bang her out until recently. How was it that he seemed to always show up in the places where she was? Were those things just coincidence or was he stalking and following her? Interesting.

She also thought about Evan. He was stupid and ignorant but not a stalker. On second thought, maybe he was. He sent her a white dove with an arrow through its breast not to mention how rough he was with her at the café. She was forced to admit that he was just crazy enough that it could have been him.

Sydney was correct about one thing: someone *was* trying to hurt her and she had suspects but no idea who it was.

Sydney rode to the Animal Hospital with the dogs and Gigi called and scheduled A Little Helper Movers in Cleveland to pack and move her clothing into storage until she returned from her trip. Her cousin Lena would coordinate the move for her while she was away and she'd take care of forwarding her mail to a P.O. Box when she returned.

There was still a lot of loose ends to tie up before her flight left at six. The bedroom door needed to be repaired and the blood on the floor from the dog had to be cleaned up before it permanently stained the hardwood. Lena would coordinate that as well.

Thank God the closing had already occurred or she would have killed Sydney had she lost the sale due to this incident. On second thought, she couldn't blame Sydney. Had it not been for her and that .357 they'd both probably be dog food right now. The thought of Syd's little bitty self with a big ole .357 was hilarious and she shook her head at the thought. Sydney. The girl was looney to say the least.

She ran back inside the condo to retrieve one last thing: the keys to her Beemer. That was her dream truck. She was so proud of herself when she purchased it. She scrimped and saved for two years to be able to write the check and pay for it in full from the dealership. She paid nineteen thousand dollars in cash for a three-year-old certified pre-owned BMW rather than fifty-thousand for it brand new.

Wealthy people were funny. They'd buy a certified pre-owned luxury car in a heartbeat but avoid a *used* car like bubonic plague.

Syd was still at the animal hospital and Gigi would soon be on her way there. She put the keys in the mailbox and called her oldest friend to come and pick the truck up.

She trusted Lashon and Al to take good care of her baby while she was gone and they could use it until she returned from Vegas. She'd then either sell it or trade it in for a new one. New to her anyway. Gigi would much rather let someone else breathe in the new car smell, pay the new car price and suffer the new car depreciation. Certified pre-owned or used or whatever you wanted to call it was just fine with her.

She arrived at the animal hospital and breathed a sigh of relief. Vongi had suffered a few puncture wounds but no major arteries were hit, no organs were damaged and no bones were broken. The veterinarian reported he went limp in the larger dog's mouth giving the illusion that he was dead and probably saved his own life by doing so. Had he continued to struggle, the Cane Corso would have clenched his jaws even harder basically crushing the Yorkie with his vice-like grip. That's why she hated large dogs and was terrified of them and their potential to do great damage.

Syd made her plans regarding the Cane Corso clear: She would nurse him back to health and subsequently adopt him. The presence of the monstrous beast at Sydney's house would mean Gigi visited less. Tim and his new found intolerance of her would be glad of that.

The round from the .357 pierced clean through the dog's shoulder, severing a tendon in the process. Sydney refused to leave the dog alone and opted to stay at the Clinic throughout the surgery to repair the damage.

Both the Cane Corso, dubbed Pharaoh by Sydney and Vongi would board at the Clinic while Syd and Gigi were out of town. Thank God both dogs had survived although Vongi wasn't completely out of the woods yet.

Sydney argued with Tim back and forth over the phone. He'd made plans for the two of them for New Year's Eve and was not happy when Syd informed him of the sudden change. His displeasure grew even stronger when he was advised they would have to pay out of pocket for a plane ticket if he wanted to accompany his wife. He didn't get why all of Gigi's expenses were paid but they had to pay their own.

He refused to take the silly little trip if he had to pay for himself. Sydney could hit herself a few times over the next few days listening to Gigi and that big ass football player smash. Then maybe she would realize and understand how blessed she was to have a man.

Tim had women on standby and could replace her with ease. The current ratio of women to men in The Land as locals so affectionately referred to Cleveland, meant *her* pickings would be very slim. She could go flying off to Vegas running up behind Gigi if she wanted to, he'd spend New Year's Eve with Dionne. He was pretty sure she didn't have anything better to do. Besides, she enjoyed sticking it to Sydney more than she liked screwing him. Didn't matter to Tim. Win-win.

Cleveland Hopkins International Airport: 6:00 p.m.

The trio of Gigi, Sydney and Oshen arrived at the airport and were escorted to their boarding area like royalty thanks to Oshen's superstar status.

The other passengers immediately recognized "Killer Wave" as he was affectionately called and a mob of fans quickly encompassed him when they were in the boarding waiting area. The nickname was a play on the name "Oshen" and the damage he did to defensive lines like monster ocean waves did when they crashed into shores.

One of the PFL's premier backs spent the majority of his time while they were waiting to board, signing autographs and taking selfies and Gigi stood back and watched him with a smile on her face. Every now and again, he'd look over and wink his eye at her. He always found a way to make her feel warm and safe and wanted and…loved.

She'd been through so much with her ex-husband: the lying, cheating, multiple affairs, hiding money, being cussed at, put down, demeaned and demoralized but the worst of it all was the physical abuse. If a so-called man of God could stand in front of God and enter knowingly enter into a 3-stranded covenant with God and do all of the evil things he had done with a clear conscience, how was she to ever truly trust that another wouldn't turn on her in a weeks' time like that idiot did?

Men and women alike sought Oshen out and he turned no one away. He was genuinely a good lovable, likable guy and she didn't think she could fight it anymore. She wanted to love him, needed to love him and in that moment decided that she would. The fear was still there but she had never been one to let fear control her and she wasn't going to start now.

Leaning against a wall, waiting to board a plane, she turned to her best friend in the whole world and said:

"I think I'm in love with him".

"That's cool you're telling me" Sydney said, "but it doesn't mean shit until you open up your damn mouth and tell *his* ass."

First Class Drama

Gigi couldn't with Charla. She purchased coach seats for them to fly to the other half of the country, with her cheap self. Thank God for Oshen and the upgrade from coach to first class which saved them all from a fate worse than death.

They would have been squished in those little seats like sardines and both women were 5"3' or shorter. Oshen was 6" and huge. He would have been the most uncomfortable of all.

"If he loves you, he will bring you gifts."

Gigi's pastor preached those words so many times correlating the natural with the spiritual. Oshen always did little stuff for her and she no longer questioned if she could love him. She was confident that she could, she just had to find the right time to tell him.

The three of them took their seats and made themselves comfortable. First Class was a first for Sydney and her excitement showed by the way she marveled over the shear luxury of it all. She felt like she was sitting in her own living room recliner with a seatbelt.

The food options rivaled those she could get from Zanzibar or Zion's in Cleveland. She was especially impressed with the vast array of alcoholic beverages.

Sydney wanted a Lemon Drop but settled for a glass of champagne instead. She didn't want to drink vodka or gin or any kind of brown liquor on the plane. *That* wouldn't turn out well for anyone involved.

"Aren't you that football player, Oshen Benjamin" said a porn-star type plastic looking woman who'd approached them stealthily from the rear.

She was so perfect, even Gigi was in awe of her fluffy breast implants and impeccable butt injections. Gigi guessed she'd had one of those Brazilian's everyone kept talking about.

"I am one and the same" Oshen replied.

"It's my pleasure to meet you, Mr. Benjamin" she answered. "My name is Lauren but *you* can call me anytime" she said and wrote her telephone number on his hand with her lipstick.

"Don't lose that, and don't let your sister see" she said nodding towards Gigi.

"My sister" Oshen asked inquisitively and turned his eyes towards Gigi.

"Oh, her? No Lauren, you've got it wrong. I don't kiss my sister like this" Oshen announced and slid his tongue into Gigi's mouth. He grabbed a napkin, wiped the lipstick off of his hand and tossed it at the woman.

"Ooops" teased Gigi, "How you feeling now, tramp?"

Lauren leaned in and kissed Oshen directly on his lips. She tried in earnest to get her tongue into his mouth but failed before he pushed her away. She stood back and glared at Gigi.

"How are *you* feeling now" she addressed Gigi.

"Let me know if you change your mind, Oshen" she said and walked away.

"Lauren" Gigi called after her.

"What" she asked.

With one smooth motion, Gigi threw her bottle of water into Lauren's face ruining her hair and her five and dime makeup. Water ran everywhere and the collar of her top was soaked. The demarcation line of her kitchen weave was clearly visible and her drugstore eyeliner and mascara were running. A furious Lauren lunged for Gigi but Oshen blocked her way.

"I can't let you do that and that would probably get you tossed off the plane and prosecuted. You might want to rethink that, Darling" he said.

"Mr. Benjamin, is there a problem" asked the Flight Attendant as she approached. She looked at Oshen and then at Lauren.

"No, thank you but if you would kindly escort this beautiful young lady to her seat, I'd greatly appreciate it" he replied.

"This ain't over, silly bitch, believe that" yelled Lauren as Gigi taunted her and waved her hand bye-bye.

"I'll see your ass again" she said unhappily on her way back to her seat.

Thank God Oshen had their seats upgraded to first class and Gigi shuddered to imagine the drama they would have been subjected to if seated in coach.

The Flight Attendant admired him for not allowing the woman to disrespect *his* woman. *That* was the mark of a good man. She'd seen countless gold-diggers like that lady before and somehow they always managed to sneak into first class trying to ensnare wealthy men who traveled alone into their traps. Some of them managed to get in an unprotected sexual encounter or two. Those floozies would do anything for the proverbial golden ticket.

"I can't believe *you* didn't get a piece of *that*" Gigi said to Sydney. She'd been surprisingly quiet during the entire confrontation.

"Your ass was wrong, that's why" Sydney replied and sipped her champagne. "How the hell can you possibly justify that bullshit? This *ain't* your man, Gigi" she said and motioned towards Oshen, "so I don't understand what you're tripping on" she said and continued.

"This motherfucker saves your ass on the regular and has proven time and time again that he's got your back at *every* turn. The damn man spoils your ass rotten, Gigi your ass ain't got to do shit if you don't want to, not even shop for your own fucking clothes because that man right there makes sure a stylist is at the ready for your funky ass!

This fool trusts you with his Benz, his Beemer, his truck, his house. Pull out your keys, right now, I'll bet you my paycheck to my last dollar you have a key to everything I just rattled off but *you* don't want him. Nah, you don't want that kind of man. Your ass wants a scrub, a rehab project and then wanna get all pissed off and funky when another bitch tries her hand. So again I ask what the fuck you tripping on?"

"It's not even like that and you know it's not" said a shocked Gigi.

"What is it like then" asked Sydney and continued without waiting for an answer. "I've watched you two together, I see the way he looks at you, the way he always makes sure to position himself to shield you with his body, the way he attends to your every need before *you* even know you have one. He's in love with your dumb ass but you don't want that, oh no, you want a motherfucker to bust you in the damn mouth and tell you to shut the fuck up. Your ass concerned about dumb shit like swirling or not swirling and height and those other dumb as requirements you have. Your silly ass is going to fuck up and miss out on a good ass man if you don't stop.

"Okay, Sydney. I think you've said enough, seriously" said Gigi.

"Oh do you now? Hit a nerve did I? See, you wanna slide off in a damn corner and whisper to me that you love him but your scary ass won't tell him. Well I'm here to tell you bitch, this man right here" Sydney said "is one fine, rich motherfucker and these gold-digging ass broads out here are *going* to get at his ass and you can't say shit because he ain't yours. So what you gonna do" she asked and sipped more champagne.

"Are you done? Got it all out" asked Gigi.

She was incensed that her girl, her ace boon coon, had just put her on Front Street like that. Her best friend in the *whole* world just exposed her and shit just got very real.

"What you gonna do, bitch? Tell this little boy you're in love with him and quit playing before you lose him to a simple bitch because you're to fucking scary to love again." Sydney said.

"Gee, baby. Look at this man. Women are clamoring and tripping all over themselves to get his attention but the only woman he wants is you. He's not *him*, Baby. Stop making him pay for what another man did. Love this man before he gets tired of chasing you and walks the hell away."

Gigi glared at her friend, leaned forward and looked directly into Sydney's eyes.

"The rest of this trip, don't say another word to me, I mean absolutely nothing. Friendship 101: Don't front on your friend" said Gigi, "especially in front of a man. And call me a bitch one more time and I will beat your pretentious ass. Do I make myself crystal damn clear?"

Gigi turned on her iPad and began to read a novel she downloaded months ago but had yet to read. That was some fraggle-naggle bull Sydney just pulled. This was going to be a very long trip.

Meanwhile back at Dionne's House

You're dumb as shit, you know that? You're so busy trying to get in between my legs unrestricted that you sent your wife off to let Al Bernard get in between hers, dumb ass" Dionne chided Tim.

"Your gums are always flapping but you ain't saying shit. What the hell are you talking about, Girl?"

"I'm talking about your dumb ass letting your wife go to Vegas by herself. This dude been sending her flowers, buying her little gifts and she's been hooking up with him on the low but your stupid ass sends her right to him all by herself."

"Who?"

"I told you she was creeping with Al Bernard, the manager for Black Ice, idiot. Black Ice is on that Tour she and Gigi went to produce opening night for. See, your stupid ass don't listen."

He processed everything she said. It was beginning to make sense to him and it was some straight bull. Sydney knew the rules and for close to twenty years, things were working fine but now all of a sudden, she went and got all progressive probably listening to that silly Gigi.

He was going to Vegas tonight and shut her party down. The next possible flight was a direct flight and left from Akron at 7:00 p.m. That would put him in Vegas at about 1:00 a.m.

He booked the flight online and got Sydney's hotel information from Dionne then headed to Canton-Akron Airport down in Summit County.

Dionne was more than happy to drive so he wouldn't have to leave his car at the airport. Akron was only about 45 minutes outside of Cleveland and if he drove himself, he would have to return to Akron and then drive the return trip back to Cleveland. That was wasting too much time. He had to get there quickly before that AB dude could molest his wife.

She chattered incessantly while they sped up the highway. He wanted her to just shut up. He knew all about the disdain she and Sydney had for one another, she didn't have to keep talking about it. Her whiny voice was getting on his nerves and giving him a headache.

She volunteered information about his wife and this punk trying to get at her, to spit in Sydney's eye. Manipulative and conniving was an understatement when it came to describing Dionne. He wasn't quite sure why he dealt with her or why he even trusted her, but he did. He just did.

He mentally prepared himself for what he might find when he got to Vegas. He wasn't a praying man by any stretch of the imagination but he was praying right now. He was praying that he didn't run into this Al Bernard person and he prayed that he didn't catch him with his wife and he prayed for himself. Only the true and living God would be able to stop the carnage if his first two prayers weren't affirmatively answered.

Dionne was still rambling. He really, *really* wished she would shut up. He leaned back in the passenger seat of her Hyundai Sonata and closed his eyes thinking maybe she would catch the hint but it didn't work. She kept talking on and on until he couldn't listen anymore and exploded.

"Dionne! Shut the fuck up, got damn. You ain't got to talk all the damn time" he yelled at her.

"Fuck you, motherfucker, you don't tell me when to shut the fuck up, I'm not your wife. You might can tell *that* bitch to shut the fuck up but not this one! The fuck?!"

He glared at her. If she only knew how close he was to choking her out, she would stop talking right now. He had Sydney trained and she knew when to back off but *this* one right here… The sound of her voice made his blood boil in his ears and she truly should to stop talking to him, she really and truly did.

He was pissed and wanted desperately to hit something and if she wasn't careful, it may be her.

Las Vegas, Nevada: 10:15 p.m.

Upon her arrival to Las Vegas, Sydney checked in and unlocked the door to her room. She should have known Charla wouldn't spring for a suite. If she hadn't gotten Gigi one she surely wasn't going to get her one. She turned on the lights and got the surprise of her life.

"Welcome to Las Vegas, Beautiful" AB said and welcomed her into his arms.

"Al? What the hell? How did you? When? What? Oh my goodness."

She sent Gigi a quick text to tell her AB was in her room. She normally would have called but they weren't speaking and although that wouldn't last long she would respect her wishes for the time being.

Sydney looked around the room and was amazed. Rose petals littered the turned down bed where a beautifully wrapped garment box lay. The flames of tea light candles danced and flickered in the cute little cups on the bedside tables they adorned. A standard round hotel table was set for dinner next to a window that overlooked downtown Las Vegas and it's beautifully holiday decorated buildings and trees. The view outside was breathtaking but AB's view of her inside was more stunning.

"Have dinner with me, Baby" he purred with a sultry voice and pulled out her chair.

He had dinner brought in from Ruth's Chris, one of his favorite restaurants. They were the best hands down when it came to steaks. He'd ordered Loaded Potato soup, Chicken Cesar salad, rare Ribeye with Rice Pilaf, steamed asparagus with onion and bacon and New York style cheesecake with strawberry sauce.

Sydney's mind wandered back to the very first time a few weeks back when she and AB made love. Her eyes darted open at the poor choice of words. They actually hadn't made love at all but were parties to freaky, nasty, pornographic sex.

She was a married woman and every time he touched her she was breaking her vows. Sure, she and Tim had an arrangement but she had never executed her end of the contract. Sydney wasn't all into the God thing but she had a conscience and a married woman had zero business making love to, fucking, screwing or having sex with anyone other than her husband. Even having dinner with this man in this environment was a no-no.

"AB, I can't. I'm very married" she objected.

"We're not doing anything, Baby. It's just dinner so what harm can it be" he questioned.

"With that big hard dick of yours it can lead to a whole hell of a lot of harm" she said with raised eyebrows.

He walked over, lifted her up into his arms by her waist and carried her to the table. They stared into each other's eyes and passionately, ravenously kissed.

He lifted her higher in the air and undid the buttons on her top with his teeth then reached behind her with one hand and undid the clasp on her bra freeing her full breasts. He gently suckled them both and she whimpered with pleasure and grabbed the back of his head.

She abruptly pulled his mouth from her nipple and wisely resisted his advances as her mind was flooded with thoughts of Tim, her husband and partner for 20 long years.

"Al, no" she said, "Stop this, please. You've got to stop" she whispered and pulled away from him. He looked at her, puzzled.

"I am a very married woman and this cannot happen between us, it simply can't. Yes, the other week was amazing. You set my body ablaze and I know you know the way you have romanced me has been like a fairytale. My husband has never pursued me like that but I am *still* his wife. Things between he and I are unraveling at a very rapid pace and I don't know why and I don't know how to fix it but I know I have to make it right and I can't do that if I allow myself to continually be distracted by you."

Sydney poured out her heart. She loved her husband and wanted her marriage to work. A relationship with AB wasn't even an option and she wondered what he might say next.

"How can I not respect the wishes of an honest woman? It's hard as shit with those pretty twins hanging like that though" he said as he licked his lips then slowly returned his eyes to hers.

"I'm not going to lie" he continued, "I want you but not just in my bed. It was love at first sight for me. Your fire, your fight, your energy, that no-nonsense attitude you possess, all of that turns me on, Baby, so here is what I am saying to you. That punk ass husband of yours certainly better not fuck up because the minute, the second he does, I'm coming after you.

"Now I've gone through a whole lot of trouble to set up this little surprise for you. Will you at least do me the honor and enjoy it with me? Will you have dinner with me?"

They sat and had dinner together overlooking the electric Las Vegas skyline. They laughed together and chatted like two long-lost friends. They shared their likes and dislikes, their fears and the root causes of them. He shared with her the reasons behind his failed marriage and she shared the secrets that were damaging hers. Their connection was genuine and real but she was still a married woman and neither one of them could ever forget that.

The dinner candles were burning low when he took her hand and led her to the bathroom. She took in a very deep breath when she saw the second half of her surprise.

The bathtub was lined with more tea light candles and gave the room a warm romantic glow even though they were burning low as well. Floating candles graced the water and floated amongst the bubbles that escaped the boundaries of the tub walls. The scene was making Sydney's triangle throb and she shuddered as she tried to regain her composure.

He turned her to face him and very deliberately took his time and undressed her. Their eyes locked on one another and Sydney slid her pants to her ankles and stepped out of them. He helped her into the tub filled with foaming bubbles and she sighed and allowed the perfectly warm water to encompass her body, then leaned her head against the bath pillow and closed her eyes.

For the first time in a really long time, Sydney exhaled. He used chamomile and honeysuckle in her bath and it totally relaxed her. She remembered telling him one time before that honeysuckle was her favorite scent when it came to bath and body oils and she was a bit overwhelmed that he remembered that.

"Heaven must be like this" she thought to herself and she drifted off into a light sleep.

"For you, my Sweet" he said and handed her a glass of Cakebread Pinot Noir. His voice startled her and made her jump and splashed him with water.

"Forgive me, Beautiful, I didn't mean to scare you" he said and sat on the edge of the tub.

AB favored wines from the Cakebread Cellars in California. Their ingredient list for their Pinot Noir not only included pinot noir grapes but cherry, blackberry, blueberry and plum as well and made for some of the most amazing wines he'd ever tasted. He was happy to see her orgasmic face at her first taste and it was apparent that she enjoyed it as well.

It didn't seem to him like that husband of hers was taking very good care of her. He could tell that she was used to mediocrity but wanted so much more.

He listened to each word she said to him about them being together and it meant nothing. He would back off for a little while and wait for Tim to fall and it was only a matter of time before he would. Then he would swoop in and get his girl. He wanted Sydney Zanchak for his very own in the worst way and he was going to have her.

"May I" he asked and picked up a bath sponge then dipped it into the water to wash her back with an Orange Peel and Honeysuckle body scrub. He had come around to the front of the tub and washed one of her legs then without warning, he kissed her feet and sucked her toes.

"AB, no, please stop" she said breathlessly.

Every time he placed one of her toes in his mouth her back arched and she sighed uncontrollably. Her pussy pulsated, her nipples were already hardened and she knew he wasn't going to stop. She really didn't want him to.

AB soaped up the sponge and cleansed between her legs. He wanted to clean every crease and crevice of her pussy because he was going to make a feast of her tonight. He would make her cream in his mouth repeatedly after which he would toss her salad a few times and then fuck her silly. They'd have plenty of other chances to make love but he was straight fucking tonight. He planned to do freaky, freaky things to her tonight and the next few nights if he had his way.

He lifted her out of the tub and carried her to the bed and laid her down on top of the thick, soft comforter. He licked the water droplets from her body and she twisted under his touch when his tongue explored her exposed skin.

He thought to himself how sweet she tasted and wondered if she ate tons of tropical fruits like he did. Pineapples and mangoes and oranges and coconuts improved the taste of a man's ejaculate, or so he heard and he wondered if it worked the same way with a woman because she surely tasted good.

He let his pants and boxers slide off his waist, fall to the floor and his thick, throbbing member popped out bobbing beneath him, then he bathed her soapy, wet pussy with his mouth. Her back arched and she grinded her hips against his face.

"Sydney? Sydney, open the damn door! Open the door!!!"

They were disturbed by Gigi's persistent knocks. Sydney got up and opened it full on naked. He sincerely hoped she wouldn't interrupt his efforts to seduce Sydney the entire trip.

What could possibly be the problem now?

Chapter 10

Unraveling Threads

2:20 a.m.

"Yo, get your girl Baby, her husband down here in the Lobby! Get your girl" Oshen urged Gigi from the hotel lobby.

He saw how much she really loved music and went to purchase a Pandora bracelet with musical charms for her. The concierge had suggested the jewelry shop in the lobby and it was there in the jewelry store that he spotted Tim.

"Who, Tim?! Tim is here right now" asked Gigi, "Oh my God! AB is in her room as we speak! I'm on my way down there right now!"

"I know that, you told me that already, why do you think I'm warning you. Hurry up because I don't know how long I can stall him."

Tim had no issue with sexing other women but his whole soul would be hurt to know his wife had been with another man. Gigi couldn't imagine the drama that would ensue should he ever be made privy to Sydney's current state of affairs, and she didn't want to imagine it either.

"Sydney" Gigi yelled and banged on her room door. "Tim is in the lobby *right now*" she yelled and continued to pound, "Sydney?!"

The door flew open and a tousled, naked Sydney appeared at the threshold. She could see AB hastily dressing in the background.

Sydney's cell phone rang and it was Tim. By the grace of God, the front desk wouldn't release any information on a Guest, especially suite numbers so he knew what hotel they were in but the exact room number remained a mystery. That bought them a whole lot of time.

"Don't answer that telephone" Gigi yelled, "let him sit for a second. What are you going to do?"

"What am I going to do?! Ain't nobody got time to play twenty questions with you. Help me clean this mess up" Sydney screamed.

The trio worked fast and meticulously to remove any sign of the romantic scene AB created just hours before. He was shoving rose petals into a trash can while Sydney grabbed a towel and wiped down the bath when her cell phone rang again.

"Syd, hurry up" Gigi said with urgency, "you're going to have to answer that phone next time. I'll have Oshen buy him a drink or two and stall him. Take all that crap down to my room! I left the door unlocked."

"Stall" Gigi texted Oshen, "Buy him a drink or a lap dance or *something*."

"No can do. We've already had two drinks" texted Oshen, "and this dude and his amateur behind is high. He's drinking brown liquor, Jack and cola to be exact. On our way up right now so get AB up out of there or this ain't gonna end well" he warned. "Oh, and why is your ex down here mean mugging me? You sure you're not still dealing with this dude" he quizzed.

"What ex and no. We'll talk about that later just stall that fool, we need more time" she begged.

"I'll do my best" he promised.

Oshen tossed back the last of his Cîroc Lemonade and walked over to Chance's table. He wondered what he was doing all the way in Vegas and why he was scowling at him like he wanted to hurt him. He extended his hand as he approached.

"How's it going partner? Oshen Benjamin. We've met before, back in Cleveland, at that little bar in Solon. You knocked my girl to the ground, remember?"

"I know who you are" Chance answered and refused to shake his hand, "all of America knows who you are. I didn't know she was your girl though. You're talking about Gigi, right?"

"I am" Oshen answered.

"Oh, okay because she specifically told me she wasn't your girl when I banged her out a couple days ago but it's whatever" Chance said sarcastically.

"Listen my man, I didn't come over here for drama and to be insulted like I'm a straight bitch, okay? You got the wrong dude for *that*, for real. I just saw a familiar face from a city I love and that loves me and that's it" Oshen said, "so all that extra ain't even necessary. Hey look, I'm gonna bounce really quick and get back to *my* girl so you enjoy whatever it is that brought you out here unless you came out here to try and make a play for my woman. In that case, fuck you."

"Business and I probably should call it a night. It's been a pleasure" Chance got up from the table and lethargically walked out of the bar.

Oshen wondered what really *did* bring him this far from home. It felt a little strange meeting this guy with an obvious attraction to Gigi 2,000 miles away from Cleveland. Interesting to say the least. And what did he mean he banged her out a few days ago?

"Hey, Yo? Let's roll" Tim called to Oshen and interrupted his thoughts. He was ready to go find his cheating wife and she'd better hope to the man above that he didn't catch that buster with her *and* he had a few drinks too?

"Welp", Oshen said "he we go."

It's About to Go Down

Syd, go to my room and AB get out of here! They're on the elevator" Gigi screamed as everyone hurriedly rushed from the suite.

AB took Sydney's hand and wondered aloud when he'd see her again. She assured him it wouldn't be long and they paused for a brief kiss before closing the door to Gigi's room.

The elevator arrived and the doors opened before AB pressed the call button. His mouth fell open when he saw the pint-sized, Mini-Me standing in the elevator next to Oshen.

"*That* can't be her husband" he thought to himself and muffled a snicker.

"Oshen Benjamin, my man" AB said and reached to shake Oshen's hand and continued, "Al Bernard, I'm a huge fan man. Pleasure to meet you."

"Pleasure is mine guy, all mine" said a confused Oshen.

AB should have been trying to avoid Tim and not make small talk. He may be small but Oshen heard he packed a powerful punch.

"I manage Black Ice so I tell you what; how's about I leave you four tickets to the concert New Year's Day at the box office window? They'll be in your name so enjoy the show on me. It's really good to meet you" AB said and shook Oshen's hand again.

"What's up, man" he greeted Tim and shook his hand as well. He knew it was risky, flat out disrespectful actually but Tim was irrelevant.

Tim was stunned that the man having sex with his wife had the unmitigated gall to shake his hand. He drew his hand back and sucker punched AB directly in the middle of his face. Blood spurted from his nose and poured onto his clothes.

"Damn! What the fuck was that" yelled Oshen.

"Is this *the* Al Bernard" Tim asked and punched AB with each syllable.

"The same bitch who's been sending my wife gifts? The same punk ass bitch that calls himself fucking my got damn wife?"

"Bruh, pull up, damn! You broke his fucking nose" Oshen yelled.

"I don't give two fucks" Tim growled and kicked AB in his torso. "You better be glad I don't beat *your* elephantine ass because I know you know this asshole" he retorted and returned his attention to AB.

"Let me catch your ass around my damn woman and I promise you I *will* kill you" he yelled.

He emphasized each word with a swift kick and the last time, Oshen could have sworn he heard bones crack.

"Where is Sydney's ass? That punk leaving this floor, her ass around here some damn where" he seethed.

"What the hell" Oshen yelled and snatched his cell phone from his pocket to call Gigi.

"Stay in the room and lock the door because this stupid ass man done lost his damn mind" he screamed into the phone. "Call the police, I don't need this shit" he yelled, "and turn the ringers off!"

He went back to help AB who lay sprawled across the hotel floor with his legs in the elevator from the knee down. Oshen knelt beside him and tried to comfort him, ensuring him that help was on the way. He didn't want to move him in the event his ribs were broken or he had any kind of internal injuries or bleeding. Doing so could make those kinds of injuries worse.

He stayed by AB's side while Tim pounded on every door on the floor searching for Sydney. He was determined to find her. Tim was completely out of control and Oshen silently prayed the Police and the ambulance arrived first.

There was no telling what he might do if he found Sydney and he fervently prayed that didn't happen.

Tim was unwavering in his search for Sydney. She was cheating on him and he *couldn't* allow that to slide. He didn't approve this guy so that made him illegal according to the terms of their agreement. Little did *she* know, he would have snapped her damn neck if she *ever* approached him talking about screwing somebody else.

He whipped out his own cell phone and dialed Sydney's number. He could use the ring as a pinner to locate her. If he found the ringing telephone, then he would find his elusive wife.

"Sydney, I'm fucking your ass up when I find you, tricking ass bitch" Tim yelled through the hallway when he remembered hearing Oshen tell them to turn their ringers off.

He'd better be glad he was a big dude otherwise he'd give him the beating of his life too. He knew he and Gigi both were involved with helping Sydney hide and plan her little indiscretion.

He could hear the sirens in the distance and he had no doubt they were coming for him. It was time to go.

"You've got to come home eventually, Love" he bellowed "and I'll be waiting when you do."

He headed for the stairway, bypassing Oshen and AB at the elevator. He briefly considered stomping AB one more time but decided against it since Oshen stood over him and protected him. Tim was drunk *not* stupid.

"I'll see you again" he said over his shoulder and ran into the stairwell right into the arms of the Las Vegas Metro Police Department.

"Fuck off me" he yelled and pushed the first officer backwards down the stairs. The second officer swung and connected with his jaw. It was so hard the policeman crushed his hand when he hit it. The sickening sound of crunching bone permeated the air and the police officer screamed in agony.

Tim leapt over the unconscious officer on the stairs and said a silent prayer and hoped the man wasn't dead but continued.

He exited on the fourth floor into a flurry of bullets of which one grazed his shoulder and he screamed like a little girl and winced in pain. Another whizzed so close to his head that he felt the hot air on the top of his ear.

That was far too close for comfort and he collapsed to the ground with visions of Mike Brown in Ferguson, Missouri and Tamir Rice back in Cleveland, Ohio fresh on his mind.

"Hands up, see? Don't shoot" he yelled like a scared female. "My hands are up, do *not* shoot me" Timlin Taylor said and was taken into police custody.

Oshen and the police knocked on Gigi's hotel room door once Tim was safely secured in the lobby receiving medical attention for his wounds.

Are you two okay" he asked. "You can come out now, I'm with the police" he assured them.

Gigi and Sydney had both taken refuge under the bed when they heard Tim banging on doors. Neither of them wanted to chance him seeing their shadows through the peephole in the door and thank God they had turned their cell phones off when Oshen told them to otherwise the results could have been disastrous.

"Mrs. Taylor, Ms. Haralson? It's the police. You're safe now, we've taken Mr. Taylor into custody."

Gigi wasn't tiny like Sydney. It had taken work to get under the bed and it took just as much work to get out. She opened the hotel room door once she wriggled out of her hiding spot and collapsed into Oshen's arms.

Sydney emerged from her hiding spot as well, a red, shaking, snotty-nose mess. She was full to the brim of Tim Taylor and his tomfooleries. She didn't want to fight anymore and didn't want to worry anymore. Regardless of what he called them, they were still affairs and she couldn't stomach them any longer.

Wasn't she the one to talk? She'd slept with AB once or twice herself. She may not have indulged in extramarital activity as much as he did but her hands were by no means clean.

The hallway was bustling with activity. The other guests on the floor recognized Oshen and took photos and video of him with their cellphones. He had to inform the Thunder organization immediately and get some damage control. He wasn't involved in the violent rampage Tim perpetrated tonight but the media wouldn't see it that way. He would be portrayed as just another violent football player and that was something Oshen neither wanted nor needed.

Gigi was positive Sydney's tenure as her Executive Assistant at Glass Slipper Media was over. She was involved with a client and that involvement was giving the company a black eye. She needed damage control as well and she knew Charla would *not* be happy.

Paramedics tended to AB's broken nose and ribs in the elevator. He tried speaking but Sydney admonished him as did the EMT. Any un-necessary talking and any movement was out of the question. He was stable enough to be moved but his condition wouldn't be fully analyzed until he had been examined by a doctor. She held his hand and tried to make him comfortable while they wheeled him to the ambulance.

Tim was in police custody in the hotel lobby where EMTs were dressing the bullet wound. He was only grazed actually but the way he acted, one would have thought he had actually been shot.

He saw his wife holding AB's hand while he lay on the gurney before they saw him. He hadn't missed that small detail and it infuriated him.

"Sydney" Tim bellowed.

She completely ignored him and walked by him like he was a total stranger.

"Sydney? Bitch you don't hear me calling your fucking name" he yelled. He lunged at her when she got closer to him and she screamed and jumped out of his reach.

"I will beat your white ass" he yelled.

She was grateful that handcuffs bound him to the emergency gurney and he couldn't reach her because she was afraid he would have done just that. In that very instant, she knew her almost 20-year marriage was over. He was no longer important and no longer existed to her and she continued to walk, eyes straight ahead.

"You're lucky I didn't find your ass. I'd have killed your stupid ass, trailer park whore. You gotta see me soon baby and when you do I ain't gonna be wearing these bracelets. See you at home, cheating ass bitch!"

He was screaming to the top of his lungs by now and he'd just added more charges with the terroristic threat to her life.

"Hey" he yelled after her, "Sydney? Call my Momma and let her know so she can bail me out."

December 31, 2014

It was New Year's Eve and most people in Vegas were busy preparing for huge parties. It was the biggest party night of the whole year but not for Gigi. She was working, busy preparing to kick off a major old school concert tour with five of the top male R&B groups of the 90's.

Their fans were lovesick teenagers and hot-in-the-tail twenty-somethings during the artists' heyday. The base was beginning to approach middle-age and were becoming grandparents, but it was solid.

Old school shows always sold out. A person could see the artists their parents couldn't afford to take them to see as kids, with a whole lot more spending power.

These groups made music about love. They crooned about how to get it, how to keep it and especially how to make it. Gigi thought about the sharp contrast between the love they wrote and sang about and the events of the previous night.

Tim had lost his entire mind. She had never, for the nearly twenty years since she first met him, witnessed him behave like that. She had been in that hotel room last night, hiding under the bed, shaking like a leaf in a rainstorm, terrified. It was crazy to think that kind of rage lay just beneath the surface of a seemingly normal person. She only ever saw him and Sydney interact in a gentle and loving way towards one another, that is, until last night. Last night taught her that when a man wants and loves a woman he had the potential to become ugly, frightening and potentially deadly if his love was taken for granted, stomped on or compromised in any way.

Sydney went to the hospital with AB in the ambulance. He had emergency surgery to address his lower ribs which had been broken and the surgical team repaired the damage with a new device called rib locs.

Rib fractures like AB suffered were usually treated with pain medicine and plating but University Medical Center used this relatively new, supposedly less invasive procedure and he would supposedly be in less pain. Sydney didn't report him to have any kind of real pain so the surgery was considered a success.

An assistant from AB's office wouldn't arrive in Vegas until later in the evening so the responsibility of making sure all of Black Ice's needs were met fell into Gigi's lap.

She genuinely liked the rest of the guys in the group and enjoyed being around them. Andre was young and very good and kind of a surrogate son to her. He was an undercover church musician and would only get better as he matured.

Most R&B musicians get their start and hone their craft in church and tended to migrate over to R&B. Church boys often strayed from their roots but never for long as Proverbs 22:6 advised. He was trained up in the way of the Lord and Gigi knew he'd find his way back eventually.

Talib was one of the slickest lead guitarists she had *ever* heard. He rivaled Ernie Isley and Slash with the way he would make that thing sing. He was a church boy too and just like Andre, he'd find his way back but right now, the man was at the top of the R&B game.

The drummer Mike reminded her of Monster, that drummer from The Muppets, not because he looked like Monster but because he made so many crazy faces when he played. Those faces made Gigi laugh each time she saw them. The man was serious about his craft.

The other guys in the band and the background singers and roadies were great but Evan Beauchamp on the other hand, made Gigi sick to the bottom of her stomach. He was a predator and didn't respect boundaries nor other's personal space. He didn't take no for an answer and somewhere in that empty space where his brain should have been there was a voice telling him that he can have anything and anyone he wanted.

She was glad Oshen accompanied her on this trip. He genuinely loved her and would protect her from Evan.

"Good morning, Gorgeous" she heard the wretched man say from behind her.

The mere sound of his voice made her cringe and she wished she could teleport somewhere far away from him. She hated to be around him.

"Good morning, Evan" Gigi sighed, "and please, you may call me Gigi. Everyone does."

"I'd rather call you Mrs. Beauchamp" he simpered.

She shook her head. He was an idiot and had the nerve to be corny too.

"When are you going to stop being so cold and give a brother a chance" he asked.

"How many times do I have to tell a brother I'm not interested" she asked, agitated.

Her aversion to him was increasing with each encounter they had. She wished one of his balls would swell to the size of an apple so he would have something other than her to focus on. She imagined what that would look like and shook her head at herself. The size of an apple though? She giggled at herself.

"I get it. Still playing hard to get I see. Okay, we'll play it your way a little while longer but understand something" he said and moved closer to her, "I want you. I want you bad, Baby" he said and traced a line up and down her left cheek with his index finger "and Evan Beauchamp gets whatever it is he wants."

Gigi slapped his hand away from her face. She glared into his pea soup green, slanted eyes and he grinned at her like a Cheshire cat. She was *sure* his tongue was forked and his skin had scales. Her silly ex-husband was the only man she knew, the only person in fact, that she was absolutely sure was the devil incarnate. One could now add Evan Beauchamp to the list.

"If you don't get your hands off of me and get your grinning black behind out of my face" she muttered through clenched teeth.

Her left hand firmly grasped the pepper spray in her left pocket and she laced her keys through her hand in her right. Her mother taught her how to make an instant weapon out of a set of keys as a teen. She was ready for anything Evan threw at her today but it was obvious he didn't understand how close he was to having his pretty face scratched up with her keys if he didn't back up out of her face.

"I want nothing; I mean absolutely nothing to do with you. Get it through that thick, Neanderthal head of yours. Anjelica Yvonne Haralson is not now nor shall she ever be interested in anything involving you. Ever. Back up out of my face, Evan"

"Gee" Oshen's voice sliced through the thick atmosphere, saturated with testosterone and machismo. He was trying not to whip Evan's ass and sully his good guy reputation but it looked like it was progressing to that point. Evan was becoming more and more aggressive with Gigi and God knows he would snap a man's neck over that girl

"You good, Baby?" he asked "or is this clown bothering you yet again?"

Gigi reached her hand out to him, beckoning him to come to her. She saw first-hand how a man could react over a woman last night and she most definitely did *not* want Oshen sitting in a Las Vegas jail cell next to Tim. His publicist had already minimized his involvement in the previous night's fray. Oshen always protected her, always kept her safe so this time she would do the same thing for him.

"Everything is all good now that you're here" she said. She never broke her gaze from Evan and Oshen drew her to him, tauntingly kissing her passionately. Evan smirked.

"I'm going to take off Love. I'll see you tomorrow at sound check" he said.

Oshen broke the kiss and turned and looked at Evan as if he were nothing. To him, he was insignificant, irrelevant and of no importance which all amounted to a big old ball of nothing.

"My bad, partner. Were you saying something" Oshen asked.

It was his turn to smirk, his turn to wash Evan's face in the defeat of losing a woman. No one would ever know how much he loved Mayven nor how much it killed him to know she'd been unfaithful. As far as Oshen was concerned they were all even.

Evan walked away, amused. He couldn't shield her forever. Her bodyguard, Mr. Benjamin, was going to slip up and leave her all alone and he'd be right there when he did. So she said no. What did that mean to a man like him? These tricks out here never turned him down so he's supposed to be daunted by the word "no" from just *one* of them? She was no different than any of the others.

He wondered if she liked chocolate dipped fruit and dialed his cell phone.

Chapter 11

And a Happy New Year

Wednesday December 30, 2014

Less than 24 hours before Black Ice was scheduled to take the stage, their manager Alfred Bernard was released from the hospital. Oshen upgraded both of their hotel rooms to a 2-bedroom suite in an effort to make him a little more comfortable.

Sydney had been by his side during the whole ordeal because she felt responsible for the whole thing. The only reason Tim had been there was because he followed *her* there even after he told her that he wouldn't.

Oshen privately believed AB brought it all on himself but he would never verbalize his true feelings to another soul. He should have bypassed him and Tim like they were strangers. He didn't get what the big display had been all about. All of that pomp was unnecessary and that's why he got whipped.

Sydney repeatedly processed the situation in her head. Things were not adding up. AB said Tim knew about the gifts he'd been sending her, the daily lunch he set up for a time, the one rendezvous they'd had. He said Tim recognized his name instantly and she couldn't figure out how he had access to that information.

The only conclusion she could come to was that Tim had a spy, someone he'd been having a secret affair with someone in her office. The only person she knew that low was Dionne. That's what she must have meant about stepping into any door Sydney might have left open.

She replayed a scene from AB's last visit to GSM. They were leaving the Conference room and Dionne looked at her like she'd caught her doing something wrong. She remembered her saying "you creeping, huh?"

Sydney shook her head slowly and deliberately. That can't be true, it simply can't.

"Gigi" Sydney yelled, "Gigi?!"

"What the hell" Gigi said and hurried to the kitchen. "Please tell me why you're yelling like somebody's killing you? Please."

"Check this slick shit out" Sydney replied. Remember I kept telling you Tim was sneaking around on me right? Okay, now remember that time I told you how Dionne was talking real fly out her mouth all like "your husband fine while you creeping" and she'll step in a door if I leave it open and all that other ole dumb crap?

Don't fall asleep because here's where it gets good. AB said Tim knew about every flower, gift and morsel of food he ever bought me. He even knew about the one time we ever hooked up like that. That's some inside shit right there. That whore must've heard AB set a date up that last time he was in the office and couldn't wait to tell, remember that" Sydney asked.

"You know what, I do. She came into my office earlier that morning like "your girl sold some wolf tickets and somebody bought 'em." I was wondering why she said some crap like that, like what did she know that I didn't and *why* didn't I know it?"

"See, she's dirty. Tim and I got into it that morning because I questioned him about that trick at the game that day. He'd been coming in late, not answering my calls, typical cheating man stuff. Anyway, he was answering my questions with questions like it was me who was creeping, you know. Trying to do some ole boomerang type shit. So I go to walk away right and he snatches me back and tells me he'll kill me if he ever catches me with another man. I'm pulling away from him you know, like trying to get away and he let's go and I fall into the vanity in the bathroom. I bruised my ribs a little bit but it was all good. So he must have called and told *that* bitch."

They sat on Sydney's bed and replayed scenes and scenarios from the past few months. How could they have missed it with all of the snarky comments, the snide remarks and the haughtiness Dionne regularly displayed? She was having an affair with Sydney's husband right under her nose.

"That dirty tramp needed proof. That's why she was taking pictures and shit on her damn phone. The *whole* time that bitch was fucking my husband. I know she hates me but damn, I didn't think she was *that* low. That's some scandalous shit. Hear me what I say, I'm whipping her just as sure as I'm sitting here."

Sydney vaulted off of the bed when her cell phone blared throughout the room. She glanced at the display and saw the call was coming from the Las Vegas Police department. She hesitated to answer knowing it was probably Tim and she wasn't sure if she wanted to talk to him. That was a lie, she was *positive* she didn't want to talk to him but then again, it might have been the police wanting to speak with AB.

No, they would have called AB's phone if that were the case so it was definitely Tim. She ignored the call and let it go to voicemail. The phone rang again and this time, she answered.

"What, motherfucker? What exactly do you want? What can I do for your black ass, huh, tell me that" she yelled.

There was complete silence. She didn't hear the slightest breath coming from the other end of the phone.

"I need you to bring ten-thousand dollars down here and bail me out" Tim said with a creepy calm.

"Wait, wait, wait. Am I being punked because you have *got* to be playing with me. You screw everything that moves *with* my knowledge, try to draw me into a threesome with a bitch, creep on me with my biggest enemy *without* my knowledge, show up at my fucking work location, assault a client, curse me out, threaten to kill me because you think I *might* be doing the *exact* same thing you are doing and then ask me to bail you out? Tell you what call Dionne ass and have *that* bitch bail your whorish ass out. Bet you thought I didn't know about that bullshit didn't you? Fuck you and that slimy bitch! Go to hell, Tim" Sydney hollered and ended the call.

She wished he would have called the hotel phone. There was no better exclamation point to ending an angry telephone exchange than rocking a phone in its cradle. You *knew* you'd been hung up on when you heard *that* sound.

"Well now, that was a rather enraged rant don't you think" said Gigi.

"Hell no Gee, I'm sick and tired of his bullshit. I'm through. Done. As soon and I do mean the *very second* that plane touched down at Hopkins on the 2nd, I'm making a beeline to the first divorce attorney I can find. To hell with him, that house, his little money, Charla and all of it. I'm through! As a matter of fact, Al?" she called.

"Yes, Baby" he said with a chuckle, "you can move in with me."

"That's not what I was going to ask you. I'm not ready to move in. Hell I'm not even divorced yet. I just wanted to know if you had an empty unit I could rent for a little while."

They all went into the living room where AB was reclining. An awkward silence filled the room. It was obvious the two of them were on two completely different pages. He wanted something a bit more defined and permanent while she on the other hand, wanted away from her husband.

She had been married for seventeen years not including the three years they dated. Up until twenty-four hours ago, she was a woman committed to working out the problems in her marriage and remaining married with no desire to jump into a new relationship, especially a committed, live-in one.

A relationship was the furthest thought from her mind. Now a friends with benefits, completely sexual relationship without commitment she could definitely do. She had needs for sure and they were going to have to be met. Friends with benefits was all that was in the cards for the two of them.

"She broke your face" razzed Oshen.

AB stared intently at Oshen. He'd just broken the man code that said men were supposed to present a united front in front of the ladies. The ladies would have never played one another like that or so he thought. He *obviously* hadn't been on the plane with them when Sydney pulled the rug from under Gigi so quickly she fell flat onto her back.

"My bad dude, but she just fucked you up."

A welcomed, much needed laughter filled the living room. There had been non-stop drama from the moment they boarded their flight and they all needed a release.

A knock at the door interrupted their momentary merriment. The four of them almost forgot about the dark clouds that hovered over their unions while they laughed and teased one another and the uncertainty on the other side of the door quickly brought it back to their rememberance. Gigi and Oshen had been brought together by the evilness which bore the name of Evan while Sydney and AB were tossed to and fro by tropical storm Tim.

"Yes? Who is it" Gigi called out sweetly.

"Whatever, Girl" Oshen said "let a man handle this. What's up?" he asked through the closed door. He'd lowered his voice at least an octave.

Gigi and Sydney burst with laughter again. They laughed at him so hard their bellies burned. AB just smiled. It hurt too much for him to laugh.

"It's your concierge George, Sir. I have a package for Ms. Haralson, Sir."

The ladies stopped laughing and looked at one another uneasily. The packages Gigi had been receiving as of late were not ones any person in their right mind would be happy about receiving.

"Ask him who it's from" Gigi urged Oshen.

"Watch out girl, I got it" he whispered to Gigi. "Who's the sender?"

"It says here it's from Evan Beauchamp. Is Ms. Haralson available to sign, Sir, or perhaps someone else who can sign for her?"

"I'll sign for it" he said.

He opened the door and took the package. It came from Que Rico Chocolate Liqueurs which was a very reputable company. They made alcohol filled chocolates and they were heavenly. He ripped the box open with his teeth and popped a piece into his mouth before he had gotten back to Gigi.

"I know I'm getting real tired of that dude. What's his issue for real? I mean what part of 'you-don't-want-him' does this dude not understand? AB, he's your client so why can't you do something about this?"

"I've told him to back off plenty of times but he's not use to a woman saying no to him. Believe me when I tell you they never do and that's why he's so obsessed with Sister Gigi here. She said no…and meant it."

"Well he's doing the most to try and impress her, that's for sure. These things aren't exactly the cheapest around" Oshen said.

"So because he spent a lot of money that means I should kiss his ass and be grateful? No, I'm good. I don't want anything from that man" Gigi said and uneasily chewed her bottom lip.

"Good, that's more for me. You want one Syd? You AB?" Sydney shook her head no. She wasn't taking any chances.

"You're probably eating chocolate filled with cat piss or some shit. I'll bet 'cha something is wrong with at least one of those bad boys. I'm good playboy" needled Sydney, twirling her hair around her finger.

"Well now *that* one was *really* good one. I think that was Banana Rum. Oh wait, here's a flavor map. So this one right here should be Apple Vodka" he said and popped another chocolate into his mouth. They all stared at him apprehensively.

"You're taking a huge chance eating that mess. I hope you're not all messed up in the morning" Gigi said and turned her attention to AB.

"Do you think you'll be okay at the venue tomorrow? I can make sure you're accommodated" she asked, trying to change the subject.

"Thanks Gee, I appreciate that but my Assistant and I have everything pretty much under control. We're just hoping for a drama free opening night."

"My Lord, can we *please* pray and touch and agree on that" asked Gigi.

"How about we drink to that instead? Dang, I get sick and tired of you and that God mess, Anjelica. Ain't nobody on that but you" Sydney blurted out.

"Wait a minute, Baby" AB stopped her, "what harm could it do?"

"Fine, yawl wanna pray? Okay, I'll pray: Jesus wept, now there's your damn prayer. I'm getting a drink, anybody else want one?"

She stormed off to the kitchen to pour herself a glass of wine. She the slammed glasses and corkscrew so hard they thought she might break something. Gigi knew there was a whole lot more bothering her friend than a simple prayer. Her life was changing and a whole lot was happening to her all at once. Gigi went into the kitchen to talk and console her friend.

"What's going on, boo?"

"Nothing. Ive been sitting there thinking, that's all."

"About what?"

"Everything. I'm really thinking I'm going to resign from GSM although I'm probably fired anyway. You know Charla has been *waiting* for a reason and I just gave her one. Almost twenty years working for the same employer down the drain."

"Don't worry about it, I'll protect you as much as I can. If she fires you, she'll have to fire me as well. We're a team Boo, I got you."

"I know you do" Sydney responded, "but the thing is I don't think I really want to be there. I mean I *am* salty that I wasted twenty years of my life but other than that, I think it's time to move on. On top of that, Dionne's ass is as good as whooped so I'll end up getting fired anyway."

"I know. That's crazy, right" said Gigi.

They both knew Dionne was a home wrecker. They just never realized the home that she was wrecking was Sydney's.

"Sis, you tell me what you want to do and I got your back, okay?"

"Well, when I get home, I'm packing all of my shit and moving the hell up out of that house" said Sydney, "but right now I'm going to go email Charla's crusty ass my resignation. Better yet, I'll do it from the airport. I bet that tramp *won't* cancel my travel arrangements and leave me stranded all the way in Las Vegas."

"What about Tim?"

"What *about* his shady ass" asked Sydney.

"You don't plan to be at his arraignment?"

"I wish I would" Sydney snarled. "AB needs to be there, *he* was the victim but I bet I won't stand by that punk's weak ass side. Let him call Dionne. Better yet, let him call his Momma."

Lockup

It was a good thing Sydney wasn't sitting in front of him in that moment. He would have slapped her sillier than she already was.

He dialed Dionne's number and after what seemed like thirty rings, she finally answered.

"Dionne, I need you to come bail me out."

"Bail you out of where? Where the fuck you at?"

"I'm still in Vegas and I had to whoop that motherfucker's ass last night" he explained.

"Whoop whose ass? Wait a minute, I know your dumb ass didn't go all the way down to Las damn Vegas and get into no shit. Do you think about shit before you do it stupid motherfucker?"

"Bitch, I don't need your lip right now, I really don't. Just shut up for a minute and listen. Can you do that please? Go to my house and get the spare key from under the welcome mat of my kids' old playhouse then go upstairs in our bedroom. Open the safe in the closet and grab three stacks, no more and no less. The combination is my birthday backwards and I know exactly how much money is in my damn safe, so don't even think about doing nothing dumb and fucked up. Get a plane ticket and bring your ass and bail me out" he instructed her.

"Who the fuck you calling a bitch, bitch? I swear before the living God I will hang up this phone and let your ass rot."

She was pissed. He could disrespect his wife all day but she'd be damned if he disrespected her.

"All right man, damn, you got me or no" said Tim

"How much is the bail exactly" she asked, still irked but listening intently

"One-hundred thousand dollars but I can walk out with ten."

"Well damn, you must have really hurt the man. You do know your wife is good as fired, right? Anyway, if you can walk for only ten thousand, why you telling me to bring you sixty" Dionne questioned.

"Because I'll have to live here until the legal shit is finished. Why do you need to know all of that information? Just get your ass out here not now but *right* now, and do not fucking cross me. You steal from me and I *will* find you and slice your motherfucking throat!"

"Was that a threat coming from some damn body that needs me? You need me motherfucker I don't need your ass. Now, I already told you about your mouth. I'm not your wife motherfucker" Dionne checked him, "you don't talk to me like that. I tell you what, call me back when you get your attitude together. Better yet, call your momma!"

She paced the floor of her small Warrensville Heights condo and thought about their conversation. If she calculated in her head correctly, he just gave her access to a million dollars. Fifty stacks at twenty grand a piece is positively a million damn dollars, Dionne thought to herself.

She grabbed her car keys and coat and headed straight to Tim and Sydney's place before he had a chance to send his momma. She could get to his house, clean out the safe and be on a plane before anyone knew she was gone. She'd go to Belize where she could live like royalty on a million dollars for the rest of her life. If he could catch her, she deserved to be caught.

"That trick is going to rob me blind just as sure as the sun sits in the sky. I *gotta* get my mother over there like yesterday" he thought to himself. He knew the instant she hung up on him that her wheels were spinning.

He dialed his mother's number and cringed when it went to voicemail. He left a message explaining both the urgency and seriousness of the situation. If his mother didn't get to that money before Dionne did it would be all bad. He wished he would have never called her for help. The cardinal rule amongst liars and cheaters is to never trust a liar or a cheater and she was both. He dialed his mother again.

"C'mon Momma, pick up" he murmured to himself but the phone continuously rang.

"Taylor," the corrections officer bellowed through the air, "time's up!"

Tim was screwed and he knew it. His wife was not coming, he couldn't reach his mother and Dionne was damn sure going to rob him. It was all cool though. He was going to get out of there eventually and when he did both of those silly women were going to pay dearly since they both decided to leave him for dead. He was not a man to be played without severe consequence.

The nightclub business had been very good to him and so had the investment real estate game but the gun game was so good he busted a nut whenever he thought about it.

He had a nice stash in his safe of a cool million and if Dionne stole his money today, which he was sure she would at least try, she was going to be dead tomorrow, it was as simple as that.

Sydney didn't even know he was in the gun game. She knew he had a safe but she had no idea what was in it. He lived under the radar and never drew the attention of law enforcement. He drove a baby Benz which they could easily afford on their salaries and their house was only worth about a hundred forty thousand dollars. They lived well within their means.

He sat in his cell and thought about the woman he'd loved for twenty years. He knew he would marry her the first time they went out and three years later, they said "I do". They raised three children and now had two grandchildren but she started tripping.

Somewhere along the line, it seemed that her "I do" became "I don't" and her life that was once dedicated to him and the kids became all about her job and her selfish boss,

Gigi. There was a time when she lived and breathed him and the kids but now, when the kids were all grown and gone, all he heard was Gigi this and Gigi that.

He chuckled to himself when he thought about the time Sydney told him about how petrified Gigi was the night someone chased her through the streets of Cleveland Heights, South Euclid and Lyndhurst. She had no idea that he was that person.

He saw her pull out of the parking lot of that church and decided to have a little fun that evening. The woman could definitely drive though, he would give her that. He struggled a little bit to keep up with her, she was driving so fast. She peeled corners like a pro that night and he would have backed off eventually but the police intervened instead.

The fear she felt that night would be nothing compared to what she would feel if she didn't get her nose out of his business. He had no doubt that she was sitting next to Sydney when he called, telling her to leave him sitting in jail. She would have never turned her back on him by herself.

She was probably dropping bugs in her ear regarding Dionne too. He knew she didn't figure out he and Dionne had a thing going on by herself. She wasn't exactly the sharpest knife in the drawer.

He questioned why Sydney kept listening to and taking advice from that man-less, lonely whore. It made no sense to him. Everything was all good though. He would deal with Anjelica Haralson when he got out and Oshen Benjamin too if his overgrown behind got in the way.

His biggest threat right now was Dionne. Why did he even fathom that he could trust her? He should have called his mother straightway and not even bother with either one of those birds. He *had* to get a phone call out to his mother without delay but the hard-leg officers ignored him. He would have to wait until that female officer made her rounds then he'd slip her some dick and get that phone call. Silly females would do just about anything for some good hard dick.

Tim paced the floor of his cell like a caged tiger. He *had* to get out of there.

He looked out into the common area of his cell pod at the television and watched footage of an incident at the hotel the night before with pride. According to reports, he'd broken AB's ribs, his nose *and* gave him a concussion. He wished he had gotten in another few stomps when he had the chance and if Oshen hadn't been there, he probably would have killed the man. He smiled a huge smile watching his handy work on TV. He hoped he put the fear of the devil in him. Sometimes, God took too long.

Slaying Goliath

Oshen was too weak to lift his head from the toilet. Every time he did, he would hurry and sit with diarrhea running from his rear. The chocolates really *were* tainted just like they said. He'd thought they were being paranoid and over-reacting to the package but those three weren't kidding.

Whatever was in that candy was hitting him and hitting him hard. He no longer vomited the food he consumed that day, it was green bile and he still had severe cold sweats and a 103-degree fever. Excruciating pain cut through his abdomen with each breath he took and it felt like he was dying.

"C'mon O" Gigi said through the closed bathroom door, "let me take you to the emergency room. You're not well."

"I'm cool, I'll be out in a minute." Oshen insisted.

"I'm coming in" she said and turned the knob on the bathroom door.

She was taken aback by his pale and clammy appearance and she gasped out loud. His skin was hot to the touch confirming her suspicions of fever.

"Oh my God! Syd, call 9-1-1."

"Go on with that now, girl. I told you I'm all right" he protested.

"You are not all right and I will not go away. You're always there for me Oshen, let me be there for you."

She took his hand and helped him off of the bathroom floor, led him to the bedroom and helped him onto the bed. She then tried to keep him as comfortable as possible until paramedics arrived. She breathed a sigh of relief when they finally got there after what seemed like an eternity.

She called the Lightning for damage control yet again. Oshen's squeakily clean image was being mucked on this trip and she wondered if he quietly regretted asking to accompany her.

She felt guilty for allowing him to eat poison so obviously intended for her. At least now she knew who the stalker was. She suspected Evan from the start although she had yet to piece together how he unleashed that big dog into her condo undetected that day. Even so, she was still convinced he was the guilty party.

There was a media firestorm in full blast at both the rear and main hotel entrances and there was no possible way to get Oshen to the ambulance sight unseen. Sydney suggested they cover his face with a sheet and prevent it from being photographed, leaving people to speculate as to who was under it. Everyone agreed that was the best plan and it was set into motion.

His physique was unmistakable and the sheet did very little to conceal his identity. He was wheeled into the middle of a media frenzy complete with flashing lights and people calling his name. Gigi, with the box of chocolates in hand, never left his side.

Evan grinned to himself and watched the live news feed of the gurney suspected of carrying Killer Wave, leaving the hotel and being lifted into an ambulance. The box of Que Rico chocolates was in her hand and his plan had worked.

He'd caught a glimpse of his her on the television screen, walking beside a gurney and he instantly got a hard-on. They tried to hide the identity of the person on the gurney under a sheet but he and all of America knew it was Oshen.

He knew she would never have accepted a gift of any kind from him but he also knew that Oshen would not only accept the gift but use the thing himself as an "FU" to Evan. The man wasn't going to die but he would definitely be in a little pain for a few more hours.

Oshen was a big dude and he could never defeat the man in hand to hand combat. A little food poisoning would weaken and incapacitate him just long enough for him to make his move on her. She was *going* to give him that pussy. He grabbed his cellphone and dialed Gigi's number.

"Anjelica Haralson" Gigi answered.

"Sorry to hear your boyfriend has taken ill" said Evan "but that's what happens because I'm not that dude. Straight up."

"Evan Beauchamp, you low down, dirty, bitch ass ni...You almost made me call you the 'N' word. Get off of my phone" yelled Gigi.

Evan laughed an evil, deep, menacing laugh and it greatly unsettled her. She could see the contortions of his face in her mind and it made her shdder. She questioned if he could have hurt Oshen on purpose and wondered if he really did send poison chocolate to her knowing full well Oshen would eat them and not her? The very thought of those things frightened her and she blocked his number immediately.

"What that fool want" Oshen mumbled from the rear of the speeding ambulance.

"Don't worry yourself about it, Baby. Are you feeling any better?"

"Hell no; I feel like I ran head first into an 18-wheel Mack truck, that's how I feel. What that bum want, Baby?"

"Oshen, nothing. He was just being an ass. I've blocked his number and that's that. Okay?"

"Cool. Hey, I'm so sorry to mess up your New Year's Eve."

"Baby it's all good. My life had been pretty much uneventful until I got involved with you. I can't *wait* to see what adventure the New Year brings."

"I love you" he said.

"Oshen I....."

Her lip quivered and she couldn't bring herself to say the words. He was everything she ever wanted in a man, everything she ever dreamed of and yet, she couldn't bring herself to say to him the words he wanted to hear. She needed more time to be sure.

It's okay, you'll say it when you're ready" he said even though he really was crushed inside. He didn't know what else to say or do. He'd just have to wait until she was ready whenever that was.

"Happy New Year, my sweet" he said and kissed her lightly on her forehead.

"Happy New Year, Baby" she said and kissed the back of his hand just as the ambulance pulled up to the hospital.

Sixty Second Millionaire

Dionne hurriedly packed her overnight bag. She didn't need to take all that much. She'd have a million dollars in cash after all and she could buy what she needed when she got there, wherever "there" was.

Her destination was still in question but she knew there was no possible way to fly out of the United States with that much cash in her bag which meant she would probably have to drive into Mexico or maybe even further into Belize or Honduras, then fly to The Caymans or Turks and Caicos or maybe she'd just stay in Belize.

She shook her head and waved her hand into the air. The clock was ticking and there was no time to sort that all out. Right now, she needed her passport and to get out of there.

She didn't like Tim very much at all. She found him to be a pretentious jerk in every way imaginable. He talked too much, bragged too much and thought way more of himself than he should have. His money was longer in his head than it was in the bank, he was a proven liar and was not to be trusted.

She wondered aloud why she wasted her time with a cheating, lying man like him. Then, she remembered: that good ass dick. The man was short and rather stocky but his dick was damn near as tall as him and as big around as well.

Dionne Alouette and Sydney Zanchak-Taylor had never gotten along. Sure, they tolerated one another in the workplace if you could call it that but one wouldn't give the other a glass of water if she were dying. The mutual disdain was just that deep.

Dionne's version of the story would say that Sydney didn't like her and treated her like a sewer rat from the word "go". She'd say that Sydney handled her with kid gloves, spoke down to her, constantly corrected her as if she were a child and always looked at her like she smelled something bad.

Sydney didn't know that Dionne earned a Master's Degree in Business Communication from Wilberforce University and her Bachelors in Media Relations from Central State.

She had many academic accomplishments in her life but Sydney and no one else for that matter, could see past her large posterior, tight clothes and plunging neckline. People may treat her like a two-bit whore but she was worth much more than a simple quarter.

Way back in the day, in the seventeen-hundreds to be exact, a bit was worth one-eighth of a dollar with two-bits equaling one-quarter of a dollar or a modern day quarter. The bit disappeared when the United States currency changed to a decimal based system right around 1794.

She smiled at herself. Dionne was almost positive she was the only person in her circle who walked around with that little nugget of information in her head. The average person didn't know that nor did they care to know but she did. She was a true dork at heart.

She tossed her carryon bag and her brand new Rubinesque that Tim gave her onto the seat beside her. He probably picked it up from one of those closeout stores with his cheap behind although he claimed it was an original from an up-and-coming Cleveland-area designer which Dionne knew was bullshit. It was a cute bag nonetheless and actually ended up being one of her favorites.

She started her car and put it into gear. For a brief moment, she paused and wondered if she could she be walking into a setup? Tim was a liar and a cheater but he wasn't very bright and far too stupid to set her up from all the way in Vegas. She dismissed the thought from her head and set out to get that money.

She backed out of her driveway with a huge smile on her face knowing she was going to be a millionaire in less than an hour. The tides were finally turning in her direction and she couldn't be happier following Warrensville Center Road through the streets of Warrensville Heights, Shaker

Heights, University Heights and South Euclid on her way to Tim's house in Cleveland Heights.

She was surprised she wasn't stopped or even followed by the police. The police in these communities were notorious for stopping motorist for the slightest traffic violation. It wasn't a matter of racism in any shape, fashion or form; they stopped you if you were white, black, blue or brown. It didn't matter to them. They only saw motorists as a way to generate additional income for their communities.

Dionne's registration sticker had expired many months ago and she used a license plate holder to hide that fact. She was relieved that she had not been stopped, pulled over or followed as *that* would have messed up her timeline. She was on a mission to get to that money before Tim sent his mother to retrieve it and she planned to be long gone before she showed up.

"Ugh" she muttered. She hated to use GPS to find anything. It took her far out of the way making her double back across Mayfield to Coventry and finally to Euclid Heights Boulevard. It made no sense for the GPS directions to take her that way, wasting so much valuable time and *that* was a luxury she did *not* have.

She pulled her car into the driveway and hurried to the rear of the house. She immediately saw the playhouse Tim referred to and wondered why the hell those bad ass, bratty kids and now grandkids of his needed a playhouse that damn big. The lot was too small for that and the silly playhouse took up a large portion of the rear yard. That was silly.

Anyway, she retrieved the house key from under the welcome mat like Tim had directed. She went in and headed to the spare bedroom that they'd committed many indiscretions in. She opened the closet door and there she found the safe just as he had said.

She reached into her pocket and pulled out the combination: Five-six-five-zero-two-zero. The door to the safe opened slowly and inside was stack upon stack of crisp hundred dollar bills. She had never seen that much money at one time in her whole life.

She stood there in silence for a long while with her mouth wide open and stared at a million dollars. She finally reached into the safe and transferred the stacks into her gym bag. There was so much money in the safe she wasn't sure it would all fit.

"Where did that miniature punk get all this money" she questioned aloud.

She looked around the modest bedroom and crinkled her nose. The decor looked cheap, like something Sydney could afford on her own without help from Tim.

She walked over to the master bedroom and opened Sydney's closet and fingered her pieces one by one. For someone who acts like such a diva, her wardrobe left much to be desired and Dionne was quite unimpressed.

She sat at Sydney's vanity table and spayed all of her perfumes and body sprays, and tried on all of her makeup and face creams like a little girl playing dress-up. Sydney didn't look like the wife of a millionaire at all. Her dumb behind probably didn't know she *was* a millionaire, Dionne thought to herself. She probably didn't know about the million dollars in cold hard cash sitting in the safe right down the hall from where she laid her head each night. Sydney truly was stupid, she thought.

The sound of police sirens shook Dionne out of her stance and she rushed to the window to look outside. She saw two police cars pull into the driveway and block her car in. Her initial reaction was to panic the she remembered that she didn't break into the house. She had a key. She went downstairs to open the front door and greet the officers.

"Good afternoon Officers. How may I help you today" she asked.

"Well, you can start by providing some identification. The silent alarm was triggered and we're just making sure this home isn't being burglarized. Ms…" the officer asked.

"Ms. Alouette. Dionne Alouette. I'm a friend of the owner, Timlin Taylor. He's in a little bit of trouble out in Vegas and he sent me here to get bail money from his personal safe. I've got a key inside that I'll be happy to get for you" she said.

"It's great that you have a key Ms. Alouette but you don't have the security code which means you don't live here and you don't use that key too often. If you did, you would have disarmed the security system. I'm going to have to ask you to have a seat in my cruiser while we verify if the owner actually gave you authorization to enter the dwelling."

"Shit" Dionne said to herself from the back of the police car. "How am I going to get out of this one?"

Tiny Tim had actually set her up. She didn't think he had the balls but he pulled off. She should have followed her first mind like her grandmother always said. She could clearly hear her voice in her head saying, "Baby, always follow your first mind because it's normally your right one." The police officer returned to the car.

"Ms. Alouette, it seems as though we have a little problem" the officer said. "We have contacted the listed owner of this house, a Mrs. Sydney Taylor and Mrs. Taylor has indicated she has no knowledge of you being in her home. Would you care to explain" she asked?

"Sydney Taylor has no knowledge of me being here because her husband Timlin Taylor sent me to retrieve money to bail him out of jail. He's in Vegas, I already told you this. I don't understand what the problem is" she answered. "Can't you verify my story with the police there? I've got a key for Christ's sake".

"Well, there's also the tiny little matter of the open safe and large amount of cash in the duffle bag upstairs. Exactly what were you planning to do with that much currency ma'am? Bail Mr. Taylor out of jail or maybe make a run for it?"

She stared at the officer dazed. She refused to say anything else that may get her jammed up any more than she already was. She was sure she was going to jail today just as sure as she knew they were going to confiscate that cash.

"Ma'am" Dionne said "I think I need an attorney."

Oh well, Tim won't be getting out anytime soon. She took great comfort in that fact. She smelled her wrist where she sprayed Sydney's body spray. At least she smelled rich.

Epic Fail

Lights had been out at the jail for quite a while even though the clock had just struck midnight.

In any type of jail or correctional facility, one day blends contiguously into the next with little to no distinction. New Year's Eve was no different than any other night.

Tim needed that phone call. It was two o'clock in the morning back in Ohio and he was pretty sure his mother was still in church. That's the only place she ever went on New Year's Eve.

For as long as he could remember, his mother spent the last hours of one year and the very first hours of the New

Year in the presence of the Lord. So he was almost certain that's where she was.

He wanted to catch her before she went home so she could go to his house and get the money to bail him out. He thought Dionne might rob him but one thing was his saving grace: he never gave her the alarm disarm code. She hung up on him before he could so as soon as she walked through the doors she would trip a silent alarm. The police would arrest her within minutes. If she tried to play him, and he was sure she would, she would actually be playing herself. Tim pushed the button on his wall to call the CO on duty.

"Matthews" she answered.

"Good evening Officer Matthews" he said coyly, "I desperately need a shower. Would it be against the rules to allow me to take one while everyone is asleep?"

There wasn't an immediate response to the inquiry. He'd try again in a few hours.

"I'll be there in a minute" she said and walked down the corridor towards his cell.

His dick grew hard almost immediately. He had to be careful though because this could very easily blow up in his face. He had to be patient, read all of the signs, interpret them correctly and make his moves accordingly. If all went well, she would be bent over the wall by the toilet stifling moans in just a little while.

Officer Gail Matthews popped the lock on Tim's cell. This inmate had been at the jail a little more than 24 hours, so she knew it wasn't a shower he really wanted. She would allow him to take one though then she could check out his package and see what he was working with. Then she would decide whether or not to give him the sugar walls later but it wouldn't happen today though. She couldn't allow him to think he was in control.

Tim walked to the showers and stepped under the water. He made himself aware of the location of the surveillance cameras and chose a shower head allowing for maximum view of Tim-Tim, the nickname he'd given to his penis. He knew she was watching and he was committed to giving her a good show. Not too long though as time was of the essence and the clock was ticking. He needed that phone call.

Gail had been a corrections officer in that jail for 23 years and was nobody's fool. She knew when one of the "guests" was trying to finesse her. The men tried and the women were even worse but she never rushed into physical contact with a guest. She was sure to take her time, listened and made the right move at the right time. Her patience kept her personnel file sparkling, kept her employed and most importantly, it's kept her alive. This guy could shake it to the north, south, east and west if he wanted but it would have no effect on her until she was ready. She liked her job too much. and refused to lose it behind a piece of locked up dick. She'd wait.

She watched him and chuckled because he really thought he was doing something. He ran the jail issued bar of soap across his little body and soaped up his pecs and abs, if one could call them that. He reminded her of an underdeveloped boy in his early twenties trying to entice a woman twice his age. There was nothing about him that she found appealing, absolutely nothing. He was short in stature, not even close to six feet. He was too skinny for her taste and his penis although fat was far too long; she hated the big boys.

She chuckled again. She didn't know what he wanted but she wasn't about to risk her job to give it to him.

"Time's up Taylor" she said over the intercom once she'd grown tired of his show. She shook her head, shackled his hands and escorted him back to his cell.

The poor thing had no clue at how gloriously he'd failed. She smiled to herself and shook her head again as she secured him in his cell and returned to her seat in the control room.

Chapter 12

The Pot Is Boiling

Thursday January 1, 2015

The sun shone brightly in the New Year's Day sky. It reflected against the rock formations of the Mojave quite differently than it did in the skies over the Midwest. It looked like a completely different sun than one that rose in the Mid-west to Gigi who looked out of the hospital room window and stood a moment to take in the vivid pinks and dazzling oranges, deep golds and fantastic greens. The morning was unquestionably beautiful.

She pulled herself away from the breathtaking view and called a car to take her to the hotel. It was a huge work day for her and she had to start getting ready.

She spent the long night by Oshen's side in the emergency room at University Medical Center. The vomiting and diarrhea had finally come to a standstill and he was stable after fighting intentional food poisoning. She refused to tell him Evan poisoned him on purpose. That would end badly because Oshen would kill him!

She felt horribly about leaving and didn't want to abandon him but her job duties called. Her work was the reason they were in Vegas in the first place and in a roundabout kind of way, she felt responsible for what had happened to him. She leaned over and kissed him on the forehead.

"Oshen, baby I have to go" she whispered. "Call me when you're ready to discharge and I'll send a car for you. I'm sorry baby but I've got to go."

"No problem sweetie" he groggily answered. "Go Baby, I know you have work to do. I'll catch the show later, go do your thing."

Gigi walked towards the door and turned to smile at him. He really did love her and she really loved him as well. In that moment, she decided to put her fears down and let them go.

Her ex-husband had her hurt so badly that she found herself refusing to be vulnerable, refusing to believe that anyone could ever truly love her. She'd kept her heart so guarded no one and nothing had been able to penetrate her rock hard exterior shell.

That wasn't going to happen this time. *This* time, she was going to let him love her and she wasn't going to be afraid to love him back.

"I'll see you later" she told Oshen, "and I love you".

She quickly closed the door so she couldn't see the reaction on his face, just in case it wasn't the one she wanted. She'd see him later.

She went over the mental checklist in her head on the ride back to her hotel. She didn't attend kickoff shows that often and when she did, it was always hands off. This time was very much hands on, more like a producer. She silently thanked God that her assistant Sydney was with her on this trip. It would have definitely been an impossible venture without her.

She glanced at her watch and noted the time: It was 9:37 a.m. She wouldn't have a ton of time, just enough to grab a quick shower and maybe throw together a bagel sandwich for breakfast. Sydney had better be ready because they didn't have a minute to spare.

Gigi arrived at the hotel and let herself into the suite. She heard them and almost immediately she saw them.

"Yes baby, take it all" she heard AB say, "Take all of daddy's dick. Yeah baby, take it all."

"Spit" he ordered and grabbed a handful of her rumpled red hair.

She could hear Sydney gag when he shoved more and more of his dick down her throat. Her hands latched onto it and helped guide him in and out of her wet mouth.

"Move your damn hand" he told her, "stop trying to control how much of this dick I give you. Ugh, shit" he groaned aloud and threw his head back.

She *had* to try and control it, she thought to herself. Her head game was the best, pornographic even but there was no way she could swallow all that he was trying to give her. She would do the best she could with what she could and expertly tightened her jaws around him simulating the grip of a tight pussy.

"Suck it, Baby" he told her and continued to stroke her mouth.

The sound of his balls smacking her chin reverberated through the air like a herd of seal clapping their flippers. She was giving an award winning performance and the applause was fitting.

The two of them were so into each other they didn't notice Gigi standing in the shadows, watching them. She'd tucked herself away around the corner to hear what was happening as well as sneak a peek every now and again.

She couldn't believe her eyes when she first saw his dick. It was humongous. It had to be close to ten or maybe eleven inches *and* thick. Even Sydney's big mouth wasn't close to being able to handle it.

Gigi slid down the wall and spread her legs apart. She could already feel the heat coming from her panties through the cloth and she rhythmically fingered her own clit to the slurping sounds Sydney made when she slobbered on AB's dick.

She stirred her finger inside her pussy alternating back and forth between it and her swollen clit using her other hand to lift her breast to her mouth. She closed her eyes and licked and nipped her nipple, wishing her mouth was Oshen's.

She peeked around the corner and saw him place Sydney on her knees and raise her ass in the air. He reached a crossed her and grabbed a finger full of petroleum jelly off of the coffee table and oiled up his massive dick. He took another finger full and smeared it onto and into Sydney's asshole. Gigi stopped pleasuring herself and stared with her eyebrows wrinkled and her mouth open wide in amazement. She watched him clench the sides of Sydney's hips and slowly enter her ass.

He paused briefly when she cried out with the initial penetration and gave her time to adjust to the large intruder. After a few seconds, he continued his cadenced movement and his dick played hide and seek in between her ass cheeks.

Gigi was astonished. She didn't know Sydney did anal and she couldn't have been a rookie the way her behind engulfed AB's colossal member. Sydney was a freak.

Her cries and AB's grunts jolted Gigi back to reality while the sound of skin slapping against skin permeated the atmosphere. She licked her middle finger, slid her hand into her panties and inserted it into her pussy and made her movements into herself match the rhythm of AB's plows into Sydney.

She peeked around the corner to see what was happening next and to her horror, her eyes locked eyes with

AB's. He winked at her and smiled then continued delivering his long and what was obviously intensely pleasurable strokes to Sydney.

She ducked around the corner and quickly ran to her room, closing the door hard behind her. She was mortified that he had seen her watching them. Would he tell Sydney that he saw her watching? Had she seen her too? Would he blackmail her or would he approach her and ask her to join some kind of messed up triangle with him and Syd? She paced the floor and wrung her hands with worry before the light rapping on the door interrupted her thought process.

"Gee? Honey, are you okay? May I come in?"

It was Sydney and Gigi hesitated to answer the door. She wasn't sure she could look her in the face, especially after seeing AB's mammoth dick in her ass. She slowly opened the door.

"You okay Sis" asked Sydney.

"Girl what the hell? How in the entire hell can you take all of that up your butt, you damn freak" Gigi said and closed the door behind her.

"It's easy. Just relax all your muscles and breathe."

The two friends erupted into hysterical laughter at the reference to the comedienne Mo'Nique and her performance in the stand-up comedy movie "The Queens of Comedy". They often borrowed one-liners from movies in their everyday conversations and this was no exception.

"You're the freak" Sydney said after they stopped laughing. "You're the one that stood there and watched with your horny ass. You were probably playing in your pussy the whole damn time, nasty ass."

"I ain't fooling with you, crazy behind woman. We got a show to produce. Can you get ready please?"

"Breakfast in an hour" Sydney replied, "if you can get out of your pussy that fast. I know you getting ready to beat off, foul ass"

"You taking anacondas to the tail but I'm foul" asked a puzzled Gigi. They shared a hearty laugh.

Sydney finally closed the door leaving Gigi alone. Sydney had been correct in her assumption that she was going to beat off. She was still highly aroused by the sexual tryst she'd witnessed a few minutes before and she *had* to finish the job that AB and Sydney's open display started or she would be horny and sexually charged the whole day.

She lay on her bed and unbuttoned her blouse. Her breasts were still full and her nipples still swollen. She reached into her bra and delicately removed her large left breast and covered every square inch with her tongue, devouring it as she imagined Oshen would have, hungrily licking and kissing it.

She moved her hand down to her nipple and squeezed it slightly then slowly rolled it between her thumb and forefinger, alternating between flicking her tongue across it and sucking it.

She placed one of her middle fingers into her mouth getting it nice and wet then slid it into her panties and methodically traced circles around her clit. Sounds of erotic pleasure escaped her mouth and her finger repeatedly quickened and slowed its pace.

She spread her pussy lips apart giving herself unrestricted access to her aching clit and slapped it with her free hand, gyrating her hips to the rhythm until she reached a feverish pace. She brought herself to an explosive peak and stifled her cries with a pillow so as not to alert Sydney and AB that she was indeed in there jacking herself off.

She inserted her middle finger into her pussy and stroked herself with it a few times then withdrew her finger and sucked on it. She was satiated but disappointed. She didn't taste the same on her own fingers as she did on the shaft of Oshen's dick. Her orgasm wasn't as powerful alone as it was with him inside of her either. She loved it when he would bring her to orgasm with his tongue and then inserted his dick into her while her pussy was still contracting.

She couldn't wait to see him later. She still needed some dick.

11:59 p.m. Sound Check, Evan Check

Everyone sounded great at rehearsal. Even Evan and Black Ice took Gigi and Sydney on a trip down memory lane to their teenaged and early twenties years. They were all excited about tonight and the added element that the sold out venue filled with screaming fans would bring. It was going to be epic to say the least.

Gigi made an extra effort to stay out of Evan's path by design. Their eyes met every once in a while but that was it. The stunt he pulled with Oshen was criminal if nothing else and she refused to be his next victim.

She was pretty sure now who the nut job was that sent her all of those weird gifts like the box of black roses peppered with snakes, who broke into her house the same night and littered her foyer with even more black roses. She was sure of who sent her a dove with an arrow through its heart, who tried to kill her with a vicious dog, who placed all of those harassing phone calls.

Evan Beauchamp was perhaps the most unsavory character she had ever met and she would be glad when this night was over. She never had to deal with him again after that. She would let him know that she knew he was the guilty party and leave it at that.

She was pleased with the radio spots and interviews she had listened to over the past few days promoting the concert. The print ads were of superior quality and she had gotten more than her money's worth. She was engrossed in an internet ad playing on her favorite music streaming service when he stealthily approached.

"Damn" he said and smacked her on the backside. A startled Gigi spun around and faced him.

"You are one fine ass woman" he said and moved closer to her. "I just can't understand why you won't let me get on? What's your issue with me, Baby" he asked.

"You know damn well why I'm not feeling you" she seethed and crossed her arms over her chest and continued, "I don't know what you're used to but I am not that one. You do *not* put your damn hands or mouth or anything else on me without my expressed, written permission. That's first of all and second of all, you know damn well I have a man. You're silly as shit."

"Let me ask you a question" he said and leaned in close to whisper in her ear, "Where's your man right now?"

He sucked her earlobe then returned to an upright position and slyly grinned. She drew back and slapped his face hard enough to leave a red hand imprint on his cheek. He grabbed both of her wrists and snatched her to his chest, squeezing them and angrily spoke.

"Simple bitch, I should beat your motherfucking ass" he yelled at her, "Fuck you mean putting your damn hands on me? Didn't your momma ever teach your black ass to keep your hands to yourself?"

"Didn't yours'" she fired back. She glared at him with deep seeded hatred. She detested this man.

He stood there for a moment contemplating her response and she was right; his mother would be plenty pissed if she saw him right now. He slowly released her and stepped back.

"You're lucky I like your ass, that's all I can say for your dumb ass" he spat.

"I am *not* afraid of you, Evan, not in the least" she told him. "I am well aware of your little campaign of terror you have been conducting over the past few weeks to try and scare me but it didn't work. I'm not even moved so guess what? You fail, you don't win."

"Whatever, girl, ain't nobody did nothing. This shit is *not* over, know that. I'll see you tonight" he said and winked his eye.

"You're right about that. You will most *definitely* see me *and* Oshen tonight and I am sure he won't be too happy about what just happened here. He's very protective of me like that" she taunted, "and I'm sure the police won't like it too much either."

"Police? Girl please," he said with the wave of his hand as if shooing a fly and continued, "where are your witnesses? At this point it's your word against mine and my word is I didn't do shit to *you* but you hit *me* so hard, unprovoked I might add, that I'm sure you left a bruise or mark of some kind. So, are you *positive* you want to spend the night in jail in Vegas? No? That's what I thought."

"I got a trick for you" she spit back and took her cell phone off of her hip and dialed Oshen.

"Dial your punk ass boyfriend, who the hell scared of that broken down fool?" he teased. "Tell me this. How'd he like those chocolates? Que Rico, right?" he laughed. "Sources say he ended up in the hospital with some type of food poisoning behind that shit and I heard that place makes some good ass chocolate, too. I even considered getting some for myself but now I'm not so sure."

Gigi chewed her bottom lip and fought back tears. Evan had purposely hurt Oshen but she had no way of proving it. She wished she were a man so she could knock him clean out. She was pissed.

"Evan, trust me on this: Somebody is going to seriously hurt you one day and today just might be that day. I'd watch my back if I were you" she warned.

Who Left the Gate Open?

Timlin Taylor needed a plan to pinch a ticket to that awesome concert tonight everyone was talking about. He'd just been released after spending two nights in a Las Vegas jail cell courtesy of his darling wife. He was finally able to get his mother to wire him ten-thousand dollars and bail him out after wifey basically left him for dead.

Wifey and her illegal side piece was responsible for all of this anyway. She knew the rules and she broke every one of them. He was going to pay the two of them a nice little surprise visit tonight so he could tell them in person just how much he appreciated them.

He was on a mission but first things first. He needed fresh clothes, a piping hot shower and some piping hot food in his belly and more than anything else, he needed a car.

He had a thousand dollars in cash in his pocket when he touched down in Vegas but the crooked police only logged in seven-hundred and fifty.

He hated the police. He had a few family members that were police officers and he loved his people but outside of that, he did his best to steer clear of the boys in blue.

He hailed a cab and headed to the airport. He briefly considered hopping on a plane and getting the hell up out of there and if it weren't for this little piece of business he had to address with his precious Sydney, that is exactly what he would have done. This time he was only going to the rental car terminal to pick-up some transportation. The desert was too big to try and walk to and from one's destination, the bus was out of the question and catching cabs on a regular basis would become far too expensive.

He kept a credit card that Ms. Financially Irresponsible knew nothing about. If she had any knowledge of it whatsoever, she would have spent it up to its twenty-five-thousand-dollar limit trying to keep up with that single, man-less, lonely boss of hers. She would have charged up too expensive handbags, red bottoms that she couldn't afford and lunch at those expensive Fourth Street downtown restaurants. The crazy behind woman would have probably tried to charge a new car if she could.

He used it on occasion to pay for his trysts or his membership at the sex club he joined a few years back but that was about it. He had never taken Sydney to the club even though he would have loved to see her with another female. He wanted to get down with a three-some at the stadium that day but she was so stuck up that skank's ass it wasn't going down.

Dionne on the other hand was a freak and always ready. One of the club's main rules was everyone had to bring a partner so there was always an equal ratio of men to women. He took Dionne there all the time and she was a club favorite of both the women *and* the men.

He turned his anger back towards Sydney. If he really thought about it, Gigi was *actually* to blame for all of this; her and that behemoth she dealt with.

It incensed him that Oshen pretended he didn't know AB in the elevator. His blood boiled when he put it all together and realized Oshen had bought him drinks probably to stall and give Sydney enough time to clear dude out. He hated a fake, two-faced, double-tongued brother. He wanted to pay Sydney and that butthole a visit for sure but Gigi and the mastodon would be dealt with as well. Nobody crossed Tim Taylor and not feel his wrath. Nobody.

He remembered AB's promise to leave four tickets at the box office for him and Oshen. AB was a bit braggadocios and probably made many of those promises and left many pairs of tickets for many people. Tim was pretty much a hustler and could convince anyone of anything so it shouldn't be too hard for him to convince the ticket counter there was a pair of tickets for him. He could sell snakeskin to a snake.

He could only imagine the look on Sydney's face right before he smacked her to her knees. No one other than his momma who paid it, knew he had been released on bail and he was sure Sydney thought she'd gotten away with her little sexual indiscretion but to the contrary. She would be as pale as a corpse when she saw him. It was going to be good.

He hoped Dionne didn't think she was going to escape his wrath either. If he got to his house and his green was gone there was going to be hell to pay the captain. He meant that.

Tim hopped into his inconspicuous rental car and made his way to a hotel. Doors at the concert venue opened to the public at six o'clock tonight and Tim figured it would probably take him about thirty minutes to hustle up on a ticket. He might have to suck a vajayjay or two in order to accomplish that mission but hey, by any means necessary.

He stepped into the shower and relaxed under the warm water. He leaned forward against the shower walls and allowed the water to pour down his body. Tim rubbed his balls, lathered up his dick and began to stroke it while his mind envisioned a naked Sydney and the way she gyrated her hips when she climbed on top of him.

He thought about how he would wrap his arms tightly around her waist and drive up into her and the way her pink, pendulous breasts would sway to his rhythm. He saw her red hair in disarray on her head and how it always seemed to fall over her right eye each time they made love. He could feel how wet she always was when he entered her, gushing like a geyser, even in her middle age and he could hear the sloshing sounds her pussy would make when he plowed his dick in and out of her.

Sydney would suck his dick, his balls *and* lick his ass. There was nothing off limits with her…except another female. He returned his attention to his dick, stroking it with intense strength until visions of his wife invaded his head once more. He finally cried out with an immeasurable intensity and climaxed all over his hand.

The quick release frustrated Tim. Sydney had changed so much it amazed him. The woman he married would have never cheated on him, would have never allowed another man to touch her. Thoughts of her moving for another man like she moved for him and her kissing, sucking and crewing another dude, drove him insane. His heart was shattered into a million tiny pieces when he saw her walking through the hotel lobby holding *that* man's hand but ignore him.

The water rolled down his face and hid the silent tears of a broken man and he screamed in agony. The noise of the shower concealed his cries and he sobbed like a newborn baby. He was in great pain and Sydney would soon be as well. Every ounce of pain he felt, she would share. That's what married couples did, share and share alike he always said, pain included.

He stepped out of the shower, got dressed and headed out to enjoy a huge mid-afternoon lunch at one of the better restaurants in town. Las Vegas was full of those casino buffets but he much preferred a real meal at a real restaurant.

If he got caught tonight, it would be the last meal he'd have as a free man for quite some time.

He pondered his plan over a glass of Merlot. He planned to leave the restaurant and ride to the outskirts of town and meet his ex-girlfriend's brother. Then he would ride with him to buy a .380 caliber handgun from one of the gun dealers there.

He could have easily passed a state back ground check and by the time the FBI check came back, he'd be long gone but he wasn't a Nevada resident. He had to have someone else put the gun in their name because he didn't have time to wait. He'd buy ammunition from a separate store, that way, he wouldn't raise any red flags by purchasing them at the same time.

He looked into buying a Blue Ice for Sydney for protection a few short weeks back because he'd never been too keen on her walking in those parking garages alone especially at night. His boy had purchased one for his girl and that puppy was smooth. It was lightweight and had very little kickback, if any and was even equipped with night sights. It was a pistol more suited for a woman but he wanted it because it could be easily concealed under his clothes. It was perfect for his mission today.

Once he got to the venue, he would start scamming the ticket agent right away. She was going to be his way passed the metal detectors he was sure would be at all of the entrances. His initial thought was to hustle upon a ticket or two but freaking the ticket lady would be much easier. He would get her to take him somewhere "private" and work her body over. Afterwards, he would convince her to sneak back to her work station before she was missed and that would leave him access to restricted areas.

He would have to be careful not to let Sydney or that bum see him. She would scream to the top of her lungs and alert security and his cowardly ass would probably run…*if* he could with his broken ass ribs.

Gigi's silly behind couldn't see him either or else that prim, proper tramp would sound the alarm as well and Oshen…well, he would just have to shoot his big ass on site.

If all went well, he would be able to catch Sydney with the bum, force the two of them to a private place where the shot wouldn't be heard and put a bullet into both of them. He would shoot the asshole first so Sydney would lose it and cry and scream uncontrollably. He wanted her to feel at fault for what was happening to her little boyfriend and beg him not to make her next.

Sydney had the cutest little feet and they looked so damn sexy in heels. He planned to shoot her in both of them. She would be forced to wear those ugly boots while she healed and after she did, wearing heels would be impossible.

He would force her to call Gigi to come and meet her and pick her up then the second Gigi got out of the car, he would aim and shoot. If she brought that big ass silverback with her, he would catch one too. Those four crossed the wrong man and they would know it tonight.

He would drive out of Vegas into Arizona, board a flight out of Lake Havasu City and then fly back to the Midwest. He was sure there would be an APB out for him at the airports in Cleveland, Columbus, Akron and Pittsburgh so he would have to fly into a place like Detroit and drive the three hours into Cleveland from there. Tim's life was going to change in a few hours and not for the better. God help them all.

Back at the Hotel

Gigi couldn't look at Sydney with a straight face after seeing her in that compromising position earlier in the day. It hurt sometimes when things came out of that area; she couldn't imagine what it must have felt like to have something go in, especially something of that enormousness. She didn't like big ones and didn't find the pain they caused enjoyable. She was a bounteous woman but those long thick ones hurt her when they went into the right place never mind going in the wrong one.

Her mind wandered to Oshen and how sensitive he was to her needs and how patient he was with her. He always took his time when he was with her and brought pleasure to every nerve in her body. He made her squirm and wiggle under his touch and feel things in places she never knew existed. She felt safe and protected with him and she smiled and laughed out loud when she was with him and was always excited when she knew she would see him.

There wasn't a want she knew she had that he didn't meet. Even after they made love, she didn't have to leave the bed to clean her private parts. He would bring a warm cloth and do that for her... right before diving into her once again.

She loved him with her feet in the air as much as she did with them firmly planted on the ground. Gigi never felt like this about a man before and it was frightening. She trusted him with her everything, including her heart and this was new to her. She'd been in love before but it never felt secure and true and right like this. He was thirteen years her junior but he loved and took care of her like a man twice his age.

"What you over there grinning about, Ma'am? That little ole boy?" asked Sydney.

"Whatever" Gigi blushed and flicked her hand at Syd. They were on their way to the venue in the back of a limousine. Curtain was in just a few hours.

"I'm going over my to-do list in my head if you must know and did you bring a checklist and clipboard like I asked you" Gigi asked.

"Yass 'em Boss lady I shole did" Sydney said.

"Okay, white girl, there are just *some* things you simply *cannot* do. Speaking like an old slave? Go ahead and put that on the list as one of them."

"Free country" said Sydney "I can do whatever I want."

"Anyway" Gigi said with attitude, "I'm feeling like I should call and beef up security. I just feel like something's going down tonight. Call me crazy but I've just got this feeling."

"Stop the madness" Sydney told her friend, "you're just nervous about being in the same space as Evan's crazy, deranged behind. I'm not saying that you shouldn't be I'm saying that's all it is."

"You may be rightbut I wish I would've taken Oshen up on his offer of a bodyguard though. You remember I told you Evan's idiotic behind licked my ear at rehearsal earlier today. I smacked the crap out of him true enough but a bodyguard would have broken that punk up."

"Oshen will too if he ever finds out about it. You pick 'em fine as shit but crazy as hell, so I know there's a little crazy bubbling just underneath his surface some damn where too. I just hope his crazy and Evan's crazy never face off."

"I know, right" Gigi said, "and you know they already have bad history so it'll only take one little thing to set it off…wait a minute, what you mean I pick 'em fine and crazy? What about that Mini-Me looking brother you chose, with his right crazy behind? I always knew there was something not quite right with that one."

Gigi measured her friend's reaction and wished she could take her words back. Sydney grew quiet and withdrawn the moment she said them. She changed the subject.

"Let me ask your nasty behind a question? How long does it take your butthole to return to the right size after that man pulls his gargantuan size dick out of it?"

"Dumb ass" Sydney said and erupted with laughter. "It's a muscle fool, it returns to normal after a few minutes, why? You thinking about trying it, although there's no way your uptight self will ever relax enough to do it".

"But don't you have problems trying to poop afterwards? I mean like can you hold it in or does it just kind of come out when it feels like it by itself for a little while. I've always been a little curious about that. Hell, I had a resident freak on speed dial and didn't even know it. I could've asked your nasty ass a long time ago. Now ain't that nothing?"

"No ma'am, I will *not* be talking to you about my bedroom secrets. You want to find out the ins and outs of taking one up the ass then you find out the same way I did and actually take one up the ass. Next subject please" Sydney told her then turned her face towards the window.

Her eyes fell upon a gentleman driving down the street who compelled her to do a double take. If she weren't sure Tim wasn't sitting in jail, she would have sworn the man *was* Tim.

She followed him with her eyes and crinkled her brow. Maybe the old saying that everyone in the world had a twin was true because Sydney swore she was looking at Tim's. She was sure that it *was* actually him not just his twin. The resemblance was too uncanny not to be.

She dialed the number to the police department just to be sure he was still there and she felt her heart sink into her toes when the control room confirmed Tim's release just after nine this morning. She knew she was in danger and so was AB.

"Gigi" Sydney said, "your concern about security may not be so baseless after all. You may want to double up on bodyguards tonight. Tim's out."

Considering Holy Matrimony

Las Vegas, Nevada is considered by many to be the Marriage Capital of the World. More than one hundred thousand couples get married there each year. Oshen intended for he and Gigi to be one of them tonight.

There couldn't be a better way for him to start off the New Year than with a lucrative new contract, a new endorsement deal, a new line of fitness wear scheduled to debut in a few weeks and a brand new, beautiful wife.

He had been discharged from the hospital a little after noon and hired his own car. She would think he was still there if she didn't hear from him and she would call his cell phone if she wanted to talk to him.

His plan would be executed flawlessly and he would operate covertly today. He would buy her a ring, select a chapel, buy her a dress and get a suit. He loved her and knew from the moment she bit into her burger at that Solon bar that she was the one.

Of course she was drama and yes she had a lot going on and yes, she was his senior by thirteen years but she was it. If there was anything that might make her decline his proposal it would be the age difference. She was a bit uneasy with it at first but he thought she was past it by now. They'd gone through a lot together over the past ninety days even though she wasn't technical his woman but the bullshit had still drawn them closer. They made the perfect team and he would do all he could to guarantee they had the perfect marriage.

His parents lived in Oklahoma and he planned to surprise her and them by to taking her to meet them before they flew home to Ohio. He probably should warn her ahead of time about his parents. He was an only child, a PFL superstar, an Oklahoma State star before that and they practically worshipped him.

His parents would almost certainly be displeased that he cheated them out of an actual wedding so it wasn't going to be easy to sneak in and out of Beggs without a huge party or reception. He may as well go shopping for her too because the high maintenance stuff she normally wore and had packed wasn't going to cut it for all of the family and potluck dinners they would have to attend over the week they would be there. She needed jeans and flats.

He looked out the window and smiled at the thought of her being his wife and the beautiful desert sun beamed back.

For the first time in his life he was genuinely happy. He was excited when he was drafted and he was thrilled when he thought he had a baby but having her in his life made him happy, like his life was finally coming full-circle.

He watched the people on the street and those that pulled up beside him in cars. He wondered where they were coming from and where they were going to, what their lives were like and what they did for a living. He sometimes would create entire stories in his head about the people he saw, a talent he thought probably developed from life as an only child. He had a big imagination because he had been forced to entertain himself.

His limo pulled up to a red light and Oshen created a story about the man in the car alongside them. In his head, the man was in town from a faraway state to visit his family for the Holidays. He imagined the man's mother sent him out for a special ingredient to make his favorite dish and that's why he was out alone on New Year's Eve. He scrutinized the fellow to give him a name and settled on Tim because he looked like a Tim.

He nervously fumbled around in his pocket for his cellphone and called Gigi. He had better warn Sydney and AB because the man he just saw didn't merely look like a Tim, he *was* Tim. He would head straight for AB and Syd without a doubt.

It was just like Gigi to not answer her phone. It surprised him that she answered it the other night when he saw Tim in the lobby. Thank God she had or things may have turned out a lot worse.

Tim was throwing a monkey wrench into Oshen's plans…again. Gigi would know he wasn't in the hospital and start asking questions. He rehearsed his answers and called her phone again. Voicemail. That girl never answered her cellphone.

"Driver, will you take me back to my hotel? I have an urgent matter I need to attend to" he said.

He thought he better try and warn the pair in person. He probably should have gone straight to the venue first considering the time but the limo was closer to the hotel. His primary concern was getting his wife out of danger. Well she wasn't his wife yet but that would change in a few hours.

He got to the hotel and found both of the women had gone but AB was still in the suite waiting for his car. They needed to talk and Oshen asked him to cancel his car and they could both ride in his.

"A couple of things I need to holler at you about" said Oshen once they were in the limo on their way to the venue.

"Give me half a sec. I need to make a couple quick calls" AB answered.

"Can it wait" Oshen asked "because it's really important."

"Okay but talk fast. I've got to make sure I have the balance of Black Ice's money before they take the stage."

"All right, well, number one, can you talk to your client and ask him to back the hell up off of my girl? I'm not feeling that dude at all and I don't think either one of us wants problems this evening because I promise you I will straight drop his ass if he puts one finger on her tonight. So please, do us all a favor and tell that asshole to keep his distance."

"I can't say I blame you Bruh and I'm not mad. I'll talk to him again because this is a conversation he and I have already had. I feel the same way about Sydney's man, the little ignorant fuck. I'd be a little nervous if I didn't know his silly ass wasn't in jail. He's unpredictable."

"Uh…about that. Dude, I swear he's *not* in jail. I saw him driving down the street in a rental about an hour ago. I'm thinking he's gonna be gunning for the two of you. From my few interactions with that guy I'm figuring he's coming in a jealous rage. I tried to call and warn the girls but Gigi didn't answer her phone. You better call Sydney and fast dude, seriously. Ain't no telling what that fool might do.

Chapter 13

The Pot Boils Over

An Hour and A Half Before Curtain

Tim sat in the parking garage in his rental car about two city blocks from the concert venue. He spotted her the minute she stepped out of her car wearing her black pants, white blouse and black jacket. He saw her gold name plate pinned to her breast and photo ID around her neck when she got closer and pegged her for an employee on sight.

"Theresa" he called and got out of the car to walk with her.

"Do I know you" she asked, eyeing him suspiciously.

"No but I'd like to get to know you" he countered. "You're sexy as fuck and you got a fat ass, Girl. What you and that ass got going on tonight?"

"Who you talking to for one and for two, you don't know me like that so back the fuck up out my face. Ain't nobody got time to be playing with your ass. I don't even know you."

"Okay, you're right. I should have come with a whole lot more respect than that. Can I get a rewind?" he asked.

He was undaunted by her decline. He'd been here before; he knew how to rebound. She was average looking at best and he knew exactly what to say and do to get what he wanted.

"I'm on my way to my gig but maybe later."

"Where do you work, if I may ask?"

"No you may not and how do you know my name anyway" she asked.

"Your name tag plus your ID is around your neck. Duh."

"Duh my ass. Remind me not to pin my shit on until I get there next time" she shot back.

"Next time? Oh, so I *will* see you again."

"Ain't nobody say all of that, I'm just saying. You see my damn name badge; you know where I work at already. I don't even know why you're playing" she said and smiled.

"Ladies and gentlemen, we have a smile" he teased. "Okay, you got me and I'm guilty as charged. So are you working that For Lover's Only show tonight because that's where I was on my way to. Can we walk together? My name is Tim by the way."

"Hi Tim. You know my name's Theresa already but everybody calls me Terri."

"Well Terri it's a pleasure to meet you. You are absolutely beautiful and I would love a chance to get to know you better."

They arrived at the front door of the venue faster than he anticipated. He hadn't really had a chance to work his magic on her and he hadn't formulated a plan B. This *was* his plan B. If this didn't play out right, he was screwed.

"Tim, have you gotten your ticket yet or were you planning to buy one at the window tonight" she asked. "You're a pretty cool guy and I can hook you up if you want. You'll probably have to stand the entire time but you'll be inside the concert and it'll be free. Plus, we can head over to one of the casinos and catch a buffet afterwards if you want. You know those things are open twenty-four hours."

"I'd like that very much, Terri" Tim replied.

He couldn't believe his own dumb luck. This girl didn't even know his last name and here she was doing favors for him. He shook his head and smiled. These women out here were too damn easy. All a man had to do was tell them they're beautiful and stroke their egos a little bit and they'd give him access to their whole world.

She escorted him to a back row seat and advised him when the show started in a little less than two hours, he would have to watch from the wall behind them. If anyone asked, he was to tell them he was a guest of hers.

Tim had no intention of doing any of that. As soon as she was out of sight, he would be looking for Sydney and the trivial asshole she was with. This Terri girl had the game twisted if she thought he was going to hold up a wall all night.

She left him in the main hall and headed off to her work station. It had been quite a while since a man showed her any interest. She was thirty-six years old, not getting younger and itching to be in a relationship. She was ready to marry and have children in that order and thought perhaps this guy would prove to be the one.

She got her cash till and took her place at the ticket window, barely able to concentrate on the concertgoers coming to her window to purchase tickets because her mind was on Tim. She told herself that she might just get lucky tonight and get laid. God only knew how long it'd been since that happened.

About an hour before show time the few remaining tickets were sold out. She thought the show was sold out months before but a limited number of premium tickets became available and sold like hotcakes. She had been called in to work to handle the expected onslaught.

At the end of her work night Terri removed her cash till and its cover from the drawer. She was excited and looking forward to enjoying the show with Tim. Fate was on her side for a change she thought and said a little silent prayer thanking God for sending him into her life that night. She was beaming when she displayed her "This Performance Is Sold Out" sign and turned to leave the small cubicle. That's when she saw it.

She didn't want to believe it at first but there was no denying that the man on the "Dangerous: No Admittance" flyer was Tim. The security department was always posting those kinds of flyers and she normally skimmed through them, never saw anyone she knew and tossed them to the side just as she did today.

Her heart sank into her toes when she saw Tim's face. She had been so desperate to have a man pay attention to her that she let this guy right in without a moment's hesitation. She smacked her forehead repeatedly and chided herself for the reckless mistake and panicked because she didn't know exactly *what* to do next. If she told security she would lose her job and she needed the extra money. If she said nothing and he hurt someone, she would lose her job and she needed the extra money. Her horniness had created a winless situation she thought to herself and she didn't know how to fix it.

Tim Taylor left his seat the minute her back was turned. Her services were no longer needed and he was on a mission. He stealthily made his way from the rear of the amphitheater towards the stage.

Visions of that cheesy bum sucking *his* Sydney's titties and fucking *his* wife square dead in her ass and licking *his* woman's pussy danced in his head. He tried in earnest to get them to disappear but to no avail and his anger grew hotter with each passing moment. He was like a volcano that swallowed all the hate and sin of the world until it could swallow no more and spewed it back upon the earth as burning hot molten lava destroying everything in its path.

"Excuse me, Sir. Can I help you find something" the voice behind him asked?

"No, no" Tim replied. "I'm straight. I was just checking out the lighting situation."

He had to get away from that security guard as quickly as possible. He didn't want him asking too many questions and picked up his pace to shake him.

"I thought they did that hours ago" the security guy said. "Say, slow down a second. You wouldn't happen to have some ID on you, would you? I see your white access badge is missing. Can't be too safe around here, especially with so many nuts running around shooting up movie theaters and what not."

"Missing? What you talking about? I got my shit right here" Tim said and rapidly pulled his gun from his side and trained it on the guard.

"Get your nosey ass over here, old man. You saw me trying to get the hell away from you. Should a let my ass go. You done fucked up, my man."

He held his hand steady and watched the older gentleman approach. He was ready for anything that might come at him tonight including this guy running, screaming or trying to fight him so he fastened his eyes to his hands and feet to pick up on any sudden movements.

"Black Ice's dressing room right now" he demanded.

He pressed his pistol firmly against the man's ribs from the rear and shoved him towards the left wing.

"If you make any sudden moves or cry out I promise you I will pop your ass; I swear 'fore God" Tim said. "I ain't in the mood for no bullshit so do what I tell you and nobody gets hurt. Got it? Good. Walk motherfucker."

The Ultimate Disrespect

Evan Beauchamp followed Gigi's every movement with his eyes. She moved very gracefully and showed great agility for a woman her size. He wondered if he was strong enough to hold her against the wall and screw her. She wasn't supermodel sized after all just super-size he chuckled to himself.

He had to admit though that she was gorgeous and he salivated at the thought of tasting her. It stumped him how a woman of her level continually turned him down because he *never* had a problem getting a woman before. He had been with women of every nationality, color, height and demographic but he never thought he would find himself chasing a plus sized girl.

Where did she get off having so much self-esteem and self-worth and value? She was lucky he gave her the time of day and she should be groveling at his feet, thanking him for the opportunity.

He watched her check in with the artists' managers, making sure all of their riders were closely executed. She was so sexy with her clipboard in her hand, running things. She was in control of everything…but him. He was the boss and it was high time she knew it.

He caught her coming out of the women's powder room. He saw when she went in and knew that was the perfect time to make his move especially since he put her big ass boyfriend in the hospital last night. He knew he wouldn't be there to rescue her.

"Why do you keep teasing me like this when you know I want your fine ass, Girl? You're *gonna* let me taste that pussy tonight, damn it" he said through clenched teeth.

He covered her mouth with his hand and pushed her back into the lounge, locking the door behind him.

"Grmph, mmph mmph" she tried to speak. She opened her mouth as wide as she could and bit his hand.

"Bitch! What the fuck" he screamed. He winced in pain, drew back and connected with her jaw.

"Bitch" she questioned as she picked herself up off of the floor, "nah, bitch you *hit* like a bitch" Gigi hissed and bolted for the door. "Help" she screamed and pounded and kicked on the door. "Somebody help!"

Evan rushed to reach her and snatched her back, throwing her down to the floor.

"Try that bullshit again and I'll fuck you up. As a matter of fact…"

He quickly removed his belt from his pants and bound her wrists behind her. He ripped open her dress, unhooked her front hook bra with his teeth and sucked her breasts, leaning in from above her.

"Oshen" she yelled, "Help!"

Evan punched her in her mouth, cutting his fist against her teeth.

"Didn't I tell you I would fuck you up if you tried that bullshit" he asked and punched her again. He reached down, removed her thong and stuffed it into her mouth.

"That should help you shut the fuck up" he said.

He dragged her across the floor to the chaise lounge, picked her up and spread her legs apart. He stood back and admired her exposed body. His hands followed the valleys and peaks of her curves until they found a resting place on her fat pussy. He squeezed it and she pressed her legs closed tightly around his wrist. He pried them back open as if his hand were a crowbar and sopped up the juices running from her slippery snatch.

He was going to make her enjoy this and cum if it killed him. She had Oshen crazy and he was about to find out just the reason why.

He sucked her clit and coaxed it out of its hood and then alternately licked and smacked it with his hand all while she squirmed to get free from his grip. He replaced his tongue with his hand and inserted one finger into her, then two and finally three. She screamed when he drove his fingers in and out of her dry pussy. He'd already placed her thong in her mouth and muffled her pained cries which sounded like moans to the sick bastard.

"Your fat ass should have been grateful I wanted to taste your pudgy ass pussy" he snarled at her, "ungrateful ass bitch. Beg me for it, beg me for this dick" He mounted her around her chest and shoved his dick into her face.

"Suck it, fat bitch" he growled smacking her about the face with it. He snatched the thong from her mouth and forced it into her mouth and groaned. That was just the break she needed, she thought to herself. She took in a deep breath. She wouldn't be able to breathe for a few seconds after she clamped down on his dick and locked her jaws. He yanked it out right before she lowered her bottom jaw like he'd just read her mind.

"Bitch I woulda broke your fucking jaw if you woulda bit my shit. That's okay, I got a trick for your ass" he told her.

He climbed off of her and roughly pulled her up by her hair then dragged her to the vanity and forced her to bend over facing the mirror. She could see his reflection smiling at her like the devil made flesh and then he disappeared from view. She felt his mouth nip her hips and lick her ass cheeks and his rough hands rubbed her delicate clit and she grimaced.

"I see you like that, don't you Baby" he mumbled with a mouthful of her ass and a handful of her pussy.

No, she did not like it, she *hated* it. If she ever got away from him, she was going to make sure he paid for this extreme desecration.

Evan opened her ass and shoved his tongue in deep. She tightened her cheeks in response and tried to stand upright but he shoved her back over the vanity. Gigi felt pressure on the outer rim of her pussy and she realized he was trying to enter her but he was unsuccessful and struggled to penetrate.

He grabbed her and spun her around to face him to enter her missionary style then leaned into her to again suckle her breasts. She lay stoic before him totally exposed and helpless with her mouth gagged and her hands bound behind her. There was no way possible for her to get loose. Then she remembered... her feet were free.

He sensuously moved his tongue down the length of her torso. When he reached her belly button she quickly drew her knee into her chest banging his chin on the way and as forcefully as she could, kicked him in his groin with all that she had. He screamed like a little girl when her foot landed on his penis and he grabbed his crotch and collapsed to the ground in a fetal position.

She watched him wriggle on the floor like the worm he was and grinned a little bit. Gigi spit on him and in stiletto heels, ran for the door. She turned around backwards and unlocked the knob lock, opened the door and ran out into the busy hall, with her mid-line totally exposed. Oshen and AB had just arrived and she ran right into them.

"Baby" Oshen said, "Baby, what the fuck?" He removed her panties from her mouth so she could speak and freed her wrists.

"Evan" she cried hysterically. "It's Evan, he tried to, to..." she shrieked and pointed in the direction of the powder room door. Oshen took one look at her and knew exactly what she meant. He removed his coat jacket and helped her into it. Then he fastened the buttons for her and started for the ladies' lounge.

"Dude, let the police handle that" AB said. Don't go getting yourself in no shit behind that dude. They'll be here in a minute."

"Fuck what you talking about, I'm taking a chunk out that motherfucker's ass. Bring your ass Evan" he screamed. "You fucked with the wrong man's woman today, you grimy bitch! Come get this ass whipping or I'll bring it to you it doesn't matter to me."

"What's the problem, dude? What the fuck you screaming for" Evan asked and limped into sight. "You mad because I tasted some of that sweet pussy? You mad because I made your bitch cum all over my face and in my mouth. That whore is wet right now, still" he said wiping his mouth. "If her old fat ass was twenty years younger and twenty pounds lighter, I'd a put a baby up in her the way I just fucked your bitch. But hell twenty years younger puts her at what, twenty-five and you at what, twelve?"

"I told you about fucking with my girl" Oshen said as he and Evan stood in a faceoff "and now I'm about to whoop that ass".

"Don't think you can just whip my ass motherfucker now for real. As a matter of fact, where is my bodyguard? Yo, Jase" Evan called, "handle this for me. I got a show to do."

Jase stood off to the side and scornfully glared at Evan. He was not coming to this asshole's rescue. Not this time.

"Nah, dude, you gonna have to take that beating. I don't do motherfuckers who steal pussy. What the fuck you gotta steal the shit for with all these freaks around here giving the shit away for free? You on your own."

Oshen screamed and rushed Evan, slamming him into the wall and unleashed a flurry of fists to his body. AB and several roadies attempted to grab his arms and stop the brutal assault.

"Fuck off me" Oshen screamed and flicked them off like flies. He turned his attention back to Evan who caught him in the middle of his face. Oshen shook it off and laughed.

"You hit like a straight bitch" Oshen said, giggling.

He uppercut Evan, lifting him off of his feet. Evan landed on his back, face up on the concrete and Oshen brutally kicked him in his side. Gigi ran over and joined in, kicking him on his other side.

"Wave? Killer Wave?! That's enough man! Get off him" a few of the roadies yelled.

It took three adult men to pull Oshen off of Evan who lay there with his face a bloodied mess.

"No it ain't enough either" yelled Gigi and stomped Evan's groin. "Raggedy motherfucker. Somebody call the damn police. I'm pressing charges against this bitch! That's why me and my man just kicked your ass!" she shrieked at Evan who lay on the cold, concrete floor moaning.

"Gigi? Anjelica?! Oh my God honey, are you okay?!"

Sydney pushed through the crowd of onlookers to reach her friend. The bodyguard Oshen had hired to help protect her from Tim ran and told her when the melee began and she quickly rushed to Gigi's side. They all were so worried about Tim showing up and losing it that they hadn't thought to protect Gigi from

The two women embraced without exchanging a word. The magnitude of the events of the last half-hour replayed in Gigi's mind and she fell into Sydney's arms.

An ear-splitting boom of a single gunshot rang through the air and everyone in the hall ducked for cover. Tim shoved the security guard into the crowd and scanned the faces looking for AB. He saw Sydney hugging on that bitch Gigi and figured his wimpy ass wasn't too far away. He was glad for the ruckus in full-swing as he came within reach of them as it had allowed him to move in quietly undetected.

"I've been looking for your ass, scruffy motherfucker" Tim yelled pointing his gun at AB. "You thought you was gonna just fuck my wife motherfucker? You thought you was gonna get away with that shit, thought that shit was gonna fly with me? Nah, partner you couldn't have thought a man like me was gonna let you just slide with a little ass whipping."

"What you plan to do with that gun" AB asked, "besides get it took from your little ass? You snuck me in the elevator but I guarantee you I'll mop the floor with your punk ass without that damn gun in your hand. I'll promise you that. My daddy always told me if a man pulls a gun, a man had better be prepared to use it or get fucked up" he said, "so what are you prepared to do?" He glared at Tim through squinty eyes and shook his head. "That's what the fuck I thought" AB said and turned to walk away.

Boom, boom, boom! Three shots sliced through the air and froze AB in his tracks. He slowly turned and faced Tim.

"Oh okay, I see you've grown some balls within the last few days. I still think you ain't shit but I ain't mad."

AB pulled his own .320 and fired off two shots, hitting Tim once in the shoulder forcing him to the ground. He ran over to Tim and rolled him over to his side. Unaware he was only shot in the shoulder, AB suddenly felt Tim's hands around his throat and Tim squeezed with all of the strength he could muster. AB frantically clawed at his hands and tried to pull them away but to no avail. He was getting lightheaded and desperately chopped Tim across his throat right before he passed out. Tim clutched at his own throat and gasped for air while AB took in several deep breaths himself.

AB picked himself up off of the ground and repeatedly kicked Tim in his injured shoulder. Tim shrieked with pain as AB grinded his foot into the wound. He groped for his gun with his good arm and Sydney kicked it away just as he reached it. He raised his eyes to look at her and she kicked him in his face drawing blood from his nose and mouth. He stared at her with eyes that bore the pain of hurt, betrayal, disgust and regret and then he took in air for the last time. His vision went dark and hard ass Timlin Taylor was out for the count like a straight bitch.

"Boom!" cracked the bullet when it escaped from the chamber of Tim's gun now in Evan's hand. He shot at Oshen and Gigi as they ducked into the open door of the ladies' lounge. He hurriedly carried her to the handicapped toilet stall and instructed her to close and lock the door. He grabbed the vintage frosted glass vanity tray from the vanity top and stationed himself behind the door.

"Boom!"

Evan saw Oshen's reflection hop past the open door in the mirror and squeezed off a shot, shattering the mirror. He heard Gigi's voice as she spoke to the police dispatcher and followed its sound. They would be here soon.

Without warning he felt the most excruciating pain on the back of his head he had on no occasion felt in his life. He turned and his eyes met Oshen who had just struck him with the heavy vanity. He stumbled but caught his fall on the handicapped stall door. Gigi opened it and Evan fell, hitting his head on the front of the toilet, knocking himself unconscious and just like that it was all over.

In the front of the building, there was a whole lot more activity in the halls than usual. Armed men with earpieces and security personnel on radios were racing towards an area backstage while the police and the S.W.A.T team was gearing up outside. Concertgoers were escorted out of the venue and no new ticket holders were being allowed admittance due to reports of an attempted assault of a female and a man with a gun shooting at football superstar Oshen Benjamin and his girlfriend, one of the promoters.

Terri's heart sank because she knew Tim was at the heart of it all and she was the one who had given him access. She wished she could click her heels three times and be home because this was all turning into a nightmare and falling right back into her lap. She gathered her things and got in line with the concertgoers leaving the hall knowing in her heart of hearts that this would be the last time anyone at this job would ever see her. Terri reached up and wiped a single tear from her eye. Her tenure here was over effective right now.

Cleveland, Ohio

Dionne breathed in the fresh air of freedom. Messing with a married man almost cost her both her freedom and her life. She prayed more in those 23 hours she spent in jail than she ever had before and God showed up for her right on time. She was grateful that her story was verified with the Las Vegas Metro Police Department and Cleveland Heights Police released her with nothing more than a trespassing violation.

She decided to quit her job at Glass Slipper Media. Gigi and that damned Sydney would be sure to make her life there unbearable and she had no desire to endure that type of environment. Sydney could have her lying, cheating, gangster husband all to herself. She was through with men. She was going to give *her* life to the Lord.

"How's it going" the tall, brown gentleman asked. "This snow is beautiful, isn't it?"

Dionne turned to find a handsome caramel man with buttery soft lips looking down at her. Her nipples puckered.

He was fine not just in a fine way but in a "Damn! He fine!" type of way.

"It's okay, I guess. I don't like driving in it and I wanted to go out tonight so it kind of ruined my plans but it's cool I suppose" she said.

"Well I don't have plans tonight so maybe I could drive you to yours and we can enjoy the first night of the New Year together. How's that sound?"

"Mister, I don't even know you name and I don't let myself be alone with strangers. Safety reasons, you understand."

"Well for starters, my name is Orlando Williams but everybody calls me Chance and if you let me buy you lunch right now, this could be our first date and our second date could be dinner later tonight. You don't have to ride with me if you don't want. You can meet me somewhere if that's more comfortable for you. You down?"

"Orlando that actually sounds lovely and thank you for understanding my apprehension. I've just gone through a terrible ordeal and my discernment is on high alert. My name is Dionne Alouette and you ain't married are you?"

Chapter 14

A Great Plan Comes Together

January 2, 2015

She'd had a long, trying day so he tried his best not to wake her. Oshen Benjamin slipped into bed next to Gigi Haralson-Benjamin and found her peacefully sleeping on her side. He wrapped his arms around her waist and pulled her close to him, inhaling deeply to take in the scent of her hair. Even that was exhilarating to him. Gigi was everything to Oshen and finally, she was all his. It had been a bumpy and expensive ride but it had all been worth it.

He thought back on that day not even 10 short weeks ago when he'd seen her in the parking lot having a spat with Evan. He didn't know if she was with him at that time or not but he knew he was going to take her from him if she was.

Evan ruined his memory of the love of his life. There would never be another Mayven and he would never have another Baby Janay. So he decided to return the favor and ruin the rest of *Evan's* life. He made him his fall guy. Genius move.

It was difficult to find a florist open late night that carried black roses or could dye them quickly but the internet made it possible. The bows they used on those floral boxes were always easy to slip on and slip off so adding snakes into the box with the roses was pretty easy. The snakes were all non-venomous and no one would have gotten hurt that night. He wanted to be her hero but not at the cost of hurting her.

It was a little more difficult to bribe the guard at the gate of her condo to not only let his brother and cousin into the gated community but to look the other way as they gained interior access to her house as well. He called the pair from the restaurant and detained her long enough to get everything set up. They had to pay that punk ass guard a thousand dollars all three times they went to her house. Greedy motherfucker.

It broke his heart when he bought that white dove and had to shoot it in its breast. The bird was a universal sign of peace but he had to commit the violent act because he needed a hole to push the arrow through. It was either convenience or dumb ass luck that Evan's corny roses arrived at the same time as that fucked up bird.

Oshen remembered to be really careful and wear gloves when handling the box he sent the dead dove in. He didn't want his fingerprints or DNA to show up on the box or any of its contents. He was Killer Wave and the bad press could have killed his career. He paid the flower guy who had just taken up Evan's sissified flowers to deliver the box he'd "forgotten" quite handsomely.

He felt most sad about unleashing the dog at her condo because it killed not only her dog and almost got his brothers dog Sugar Shane killed as well. His brother loved that big dumb dog and was sick when he couldn't retrieve it. Sydney ended up adopting Sugar Shane, renamed him Pharaoh and paid all of his vet bills.

Vongi eventually succumbed to his wounds and went to his final resting place. Gigi was a complete emotional mess after that. She slept in his arms each night following his departure and he often had to wipe her tears as she drifted off to sleep. It was never his intention to hurt her. He only meant to scare her, to drive her into his arms, to set himself up as the hero and get her to trust him but never did he mean to hurt her.

He offered to replace the Yorkie with a Bichon Frise but she declined the offer. Vongi was like a baby to her and her heart hurt far too greatly to consider replacing him right now. He would have to give her time on that one.

After Evan sent those chocolates and sent him to the hospital, Gigi was convinced all the other stuff was him too. The way she looked at him had changed. She began to look at him the way he always looked at her.

She was finally in love with him and she was his wife. He prayed she never found out it'd been him all along doing those horrible things to her and scaring the shit out of her. He would lose her lightning strike quick if she *ever* found out. He had to prevent that from happening at all costs.

He'd proven himself to be everything she thought she wanted and saving her from that butthole tonight cemented it

Oshen was happy and satisfied with Gigi laying in his arms. His work was done and he got his girl. She had been created for him and he was glad he made the decision to make her his wife. He was even happier that she had agreed. Everyone in his circle would be pleased too but surprised.

She was never officially his girl so they would be shocked to hear that they'd married.

He was the first man she'd ever been with that wasn't black and she was the first woman he'd ever been with that wasn't white. He wasn't sure what his parents' true reaction to her would be just as he wasn't sure how her family would react to him. Interracial relationships and marriages were far more acceptable today than they ever had been but there were still some with an aversion to the idea. He hoped their families weren't in that number.

He fondled her breasts from behind and grinded his hips against her heart shaped bottom. It was soft and juicy and he loved the way it felt against his dick. He opened her pussy lips and slid his rock solid dick into her with relative ease. That was another one of the things he loved about her: she was always ready to receive him.

She moaned in her sleep and whispered his name then moved her hips backwards to take in all of him. He wasn't a particularly large man when it came to penis size but the six or seven inches he brought to the table was more than enough to stuff her full.

He grasped her hips as they began their erotic dance. The very expensive bed creaked with each pump into her and she cried out with pleasure in response. He plunged deep inside of her, over and over again, sucked on her ear lobe and nibbled her neck. Oshen held her in place with one arm around her waist and fondled her hefty breasts with his free hand. He rubbed her nipples between his thumb and forefinger and she gasped with desire. He pulled out of her and turned her on her back to gaze into her eyes. He didn't want to see her from behind, he wanted to see her face every time he drove into her.

"Give me my damn pussy, Mrs. Benjamin" he whispered in her ear and glided into her again. She dug her fingernails into his back and bit his shoulder to suppress her scream and he thrusted into her over and over again. He straightened his back and watched her breasts jump each time he stroked her and bent his head down to catch them in his mouth and felt her rake her nails down his back.

"Fuck this pussy, Mr. Benjamin. Fuck the shit out of your wife, damn it." she ordered Oshen.

He returned to an upright position and put both of her legs over his shoulders. He watched his pink dick as it moved in and out of her brown, bare pussy at a heated pace and the sound of the headboard banging against the wall to his tempo pushed him to pound into her more. She took control and rolled on top of him. He hooked his hands under her arms and gripped her shoulders ramming upwards into her with an unheralded intensity and she pleaded with him to hammer her sloshing wet pussy harder. She screamed his name each time his skin slapped against hers until he crested and jam-packed her to the rim with his seed and collapsed on top of her.

He listened to her heart beat in sync with his and smiled while his spent dick lay flaccid inside of her. It had been a long journey and he was ecstatic that she lay in his arms as his wife. She proved herself to be a ride or die for him on two separate occasions. Had it not been for her intervention, Evan may have gotten them both.

They were like a professional wrestling tag-team tonight. He tagged her in and when he jabbed, she jabbed, when he kicked, she kicked. He needed a woman like that in his life and he was elated that it was her.

It felt good to see Evan Beauchamp taken away in handcuffs. He was charged with discharging a firearm in a public place and attempted felonious assault, both felonies.

He wasn't being charged with assaulting Gigi because she and Oshen whipped him so badly they risked being charged with felonious assault as well. When the police asked Gigi if she wanted to press charges she looked at Evan and asked him "*Do* I?" Had he pressed charges against her and Oshen, she would have returned the favor and pressed them against him. They do nasty, nasty things to rapists in prison and he would have had to register as a sex offender for the rest of his life. They let him walk on the sexual assault but everyone involved would know they whipped his ass.

Oshen was concerned that Gigi wouldn't properly process what happened to her tonight but she seemed to be handling it well. It may come out later and it could very well be ugly but he was resolved to being there for her whenever it did, however it did.

Sydney and AB were again at the hospital. He reinjured his broken ribs during the fight with Tim and once the Percocet had worn off, he felt the pain with a vengeance.

Tim had come dangerously close to shooting AB and had Sydney not kicked the gun away when she did, their story might have had a different ending. Oshen thought they were a good couple and should stay together but that remained to be seen.

"Are you glad you married me, Baby" he asked Gigi and planted light kisses on her neck.

"I am" she responded, "but I need to tell you something."

"Good or bad" he asked, pulling up on his forearms.

He stared at her intently. What could she have to tell him now that she couldn't have told him before he married her? He waited with baited breath.

"You're not going to fuck me like every day and night, Sir. I'm putting you on restriction. You can have it either in the morning or the last thing at night but I won't be able to do anything else if you keep up this pace" she said.

"Wait. Say what now?"

"Oshen, I'm serious. I'd never make it to work messing with you" she answered.

"Your husband is a multi-millionaire, Baby. You don't have to work and don't think I don't know you didn't cum. I got you, Girl" he told her and his limp dick regained its rigor inside of her and he made love to his wife once again.

ABOUT THE AUTHOR

Arya Phoenix hails from Cleveland, Ohio. She is a mother of 5 and grandmother of 2.

She has written, directed and produced a musical stage play "Changing Faces: Nothing Is as It Seems" in 2013.

This is her rookie novel and her anticipated 2nd work has a Winter 2016 release date

Follow Arya on Twitter @fantabulous_arya or Facebook at Arya Phoenix – Author.